ALSO IN VIKING KESTREL BY ROBIN KLEIN

*People Might Hear You*
*Hating Alison Ashley*
*Halfway Across the Galaxy and Turn Left*
*Games . . .*
*Laurie Loved Me Best*
*Against the Odds*

# ROBIN KLEIN

# CAME BACK TO SHOW YOU I COULD FLY

VIKING KESTREL

Viking Kestrel
Penguin Books Australia Ltd
487 Maroondah Highway, PO Box 257
Ringwood, Victoria, 3134, Australia
Penguin Books Ltd
Harmondsworth, Middlesex, England
Viking Penguin Inc.
40 West 23rd Street, New York, NY 10010, USA
Penguin Books Canada Limited
2801 John Street, Markham, Ontario, Canada, L3R 1B4
Penguin Books (N.Z.) Ltd
182-190 Wairau Road, Auckland 10, New Zealand

First published in 1989 by Viking

Typeset in 12/14 pt Goudy by Midland Typesetters, Maryborough, Victoria.
Made and printed in Australia by Australian Print Group, Maryborough, Victoria.

CIP

Klein, Robin, 1936-
Came back to show you I could fly.

ISBN 0 670 82901 3.

I. Title.

A823'.3

The publishers wish to thank Music Sales Pty Ltd for their
assistance in reproducing the lyrics, which appear
on pages 58, 59 and 109, from the song 'From The Inside',
composed by Artie Wayne.

© Copyright Almo Music Corp.
For Australia and New Zealand: Rondor Music (Australia) Pty Ltd.

Every effort has been made to trace joint copyright holders.
As this has proved impossible the publishers would like to hear
from any owner not here acknowledged.

For Phoebe

SEYMOUR HAD BEEN AWAKE since sunrise and was watching the stumbling hands of the clock so he could legitimately get out of bed. Seven-fifteen to the exact second was when Thelma began her day, and she'd made it clear that his being there mustn't interfere with her routine. She'd given him the back room, which wasn't really a proper one, just a small fibro-cement extension tacked on to the kitchen. Summer clung like thick cellulose wrapping to its iron roof, and even at this early hour he was sweating. Yesterday's stored heat undulated from the concrete yard outside, and he lay in clammy pyjamas and outstared the clock. At ten minutes past seven he sprang thankfully out of bed and went into the kitchen to make Thelma a morning cup of tea. He wasn't being ingratiating – it was just something his mother had told him to do before she left, and Seymour had a quiet and biddable nature.

'Thelma's not young and she's got that full-time job,' his mother had said. 'It's very kind of her to help us out like this, so you mustn't give her any cause to regret it. You be a big help round the house while you're there, Seymour. There's no need to tell you to watch your manners, I can say that for you. Take her a cup of tea first thing in the mornings, she's never had anyone to do that for her. I'm sure she'd appreciate it.'

He didn't mind making anyone an early morning cup of tea, but it was a nerve-wracking business in this particular kitchen, where even inanimate objects like cannisters seemed capable of disapproval if you put them back in the wrong places. Here there was a place for everything and everything in its rightful place. The tea, for instance, was kept in a green plastic caddy with its own little measuring ladle, and you somehow didn't dare use any other spoon. He took the cup of tea along the hall and knocked on Thelma's bedroom door.

'Come in, Seymour, and don't bang so loud, you'll have the plaster flaking off the walls.'

Her voice sounded tart and rebuffing, but he knew it wasn't aimed at him in particular. She spoke like that to everyone, and after two days of staying there, he was slowly learning not to duck his head with alarm every time she addressed him. She didn't thank him for making the tea, just watched sharply as he set it down on the bedside table next to her reading glasses. The room was spotlessly tidy and so was Thelma, as though she'd slept perfectly flat on her back all night. Her hair was a neat steel-grey helmet, and there wasn't one crease in the bedspread. Even her wrinkles looked regimented.

Seymour didn't quite know what to do while she was sipping the tea – whether to go, which seemed rude, or stay there, although Thelma wasn't the type of person who went in for early morning banter. Or conversation

2

of any kind at all, really. He hovered self-consciously at the end of the bed, running the sole of one foot on the calf of the other leg, aware of the trapped heat even in this room which the sun hadn't yet reached. Thelma didn't leave her windows open at night, despite the thickly meshed security screens.

'You put a little too much milk in,' she said, setting down the rose-patterned cup. 'Milk's very expensive now, Seymour. I don't want you getting into the habit of drowning your breakfast cereal in it, either, like you did yesterday. Your father probably lets you get into spendthrift habits like that when you stay with him, but that's beside the point. Oh, and your mattress, that's another thing. It's got to be turned every day without fail when you make your bed. I notice you didn't do it yesterday. And that little mat by your bed – remember to shake it out every morning and hang it over the clothesline, but don't go putting a peg in the middle where it'll leave a mark.'

Seymour nodded resignedly at each instruction and finally she reached for her dressing-gown, folded as stiffly as an ironing board across the end of her bed, and he was free to escape. Only you couldn't really call it escape – there wasn't really any private space in that tiny house. He had a quick shower, because three minutes was the time limit Thelma had stipulated, then put on a clean shirt, jeans and the hated leather sandals she was making him wear because she said gym shoes were unhygienic in the middle of summer. He attended to his bed and went outside to hang up the mat.

Thelma's back garden reflected the immaculate tidiness of the house. Even the grass blades on the patch of lawn seemed to grow slantwise in the same direction. A pebbled concrete path led to the gate in the alleyway fence, pointlessly, for the gate was never opened. It had strong bolts at the top and bottom, and also a padlock for extra security. Thelma wouldn't dream of setting foot in the alleyway. Her house faced on to Victoria Road, which was respectable, but the houses on the far side of the alley belonged to Sparrow Street, which in her opinion definitely was not. There were no flower beds, just a line of papery hydrangeas, a pallid grey-blue like old school socks. The rubbish bin had Thelma's house number stencilled on its side in big letters, like a threat of legal action if anyone dared steal it. Seymour felt depressed, looking around at the so-called garden.

Thelma summoned him for breakfast and watched keenly while he poured milk over his Cornflakes. 'Tonight I might be a bit late,' she said. 'I've got a chiropody appointment straight after work, so round about five-thirty you could make yourself useful. Peel some potatoes and put them on to simmer. You can make sandwiches for your lunch, there's cheese and tomatoes in the fridge.'

'Thanks, that'll do fine,' Seymour said, though he detested cheese and tomato sandwiches.

'I hope you won't just laze around all day. You should really spend the time catching up on your school work for when term starts again. That last report of yours wasn't anything to be proud about, was it? Your mum showed it to me. I know it's not altogether your fault, your father butting in and causing as much upset as he can, but there's never any excuse for laziness. You want to knuckle down and make something of yourself. Your poor mother, what she's been through these last two years, you don't want to add to her troubles by bringing home bad school reports like that one, do you? All the sacrifices she's made . . .'

Seymour kept his eyes on his plate. He didn't want to be reminded of all those sacrifices. It was as painful as listening to some creaky old tape played over and over, rewound when it reached the end and set in motion again.

'She might call over to see you Friday night,' Thelma said. 'I don't think it's very wise, myself. You never know if *he's* having her followed. I certainly wouldn't put it past him. She should go to court and get the whole thing sorted out once and for all, proper rights of custody, that's what she should apply for. If he finds out you're staying here in Victoria Road, he can come in and take you away, and there's not a thing I can do. I'm just a bystander, not even a relation.'

Seymour thought of his weak-willed father engaged in a confrontation with Thelma, and knew very well who'd come off second-best. But he'd had eleven years of experience in the futility of arguing with adults or expecting his opinions to be listened to. He put the spoon neatly in the bowl and carried it to the sink.

'I'd be so embarrassed if he turned up making a scene. Victoria Road's a quiet, decent street and I've got a good name here. Remember you're not to go anywhere out the front, and if there's a ring at the door while I'm out, you're not even to answer it. I just wouldn't know what to say to your mother if he turned up here and made off with you again, when she's relying on me to look after you for the school holidays. Oh, it's such a worry . . . Mind you, I don't want you thinking I feel put upon, even though that doctor up at the clinic said I should avoid stress with my blood pressure being the way it is. I'm not one to turn my back on people in need and I know your mum's got no one else to turn to. You certainly couldn't very well stay in the flat with her out at work all day and him knowing the address. Well now, I'm off to work myself, and you should find plenty to do with catching up on your studies. If you want to sit in the lounge room, make sure you wash your hands before you go in there, young man, and don't touch the photo albums or anything in the china cabinet.'

Seymour replaced the front door safety-chain as instructed, and watched through the stained-glass panel as Thelma walked briskly down the path. She clicked the iron gate shut behind her, glared at a stray dog that was lifting its leg against her privet hedge, and walked up to the corner of Victoria Road to catch the city tram. Seymour looked through all the stained-glass panels in turn, decided that even a rose-tinted Victoria Road was just as boring as amber or peacock blue, and wandered back to the kitchen. He washed all the breakfast things and put them away, peeled the potatoes to get that task over with and covered them with cold water in a saucepan. Then he went and sat on his bed, despairing, wondering how to fill the hours of the third long day. He'd already glanced through the stock of books in the living room, uninteresting books, most of them with old thick pages like blotting paper, unpleasant to the touch. There was a television set in there, but the controls were temperamental and he didn't like to fiddle about with them and perhaps make the reception worse. Thelma was devoted to her ritual of evening viewing.

He had none of his own things with him, apart from a few changes of clothing. Some of his stuff was with his father in the caravan park and the rest was packed away in storage boxes while his mother was making arrangements to move from the flat. Starting from next month she had a new job as a live-in housekeeper, with accommodation provided for the two of them – herself and Seymour. It was a temporary job, and after that they'd have to wait and see what turned up. Everything was always temporary, always in a state of flux. He supposed dully that one day the tiresome see-saw of his life would stabilise, and he'd know for certain just where he was supposed to live, and with whom. Meanwhile he'd been parked with crabby old Thelma, and had to make the best of it. As she'd said, she wasn't even a proper relation, just someone who'd once formed a casual and tenuous acquaintance with his mother through some church group. His mother, he realised with shame, was adept at imposing upon people and making them feel sorry for her. In reality, she didn't need that sort of help from anyone. It was all a pose, the act she put on. Behind her disguise of pastel-framed glasses, floral dresses and thin martyred face, she was a born survivor, as tough as any street fighter.

The little back room became even more stifling as the sun sizzled across the concrete path. It was pointless trying to open the window for a breath of fresh air. There was no movement of air, nothing stirring at all out in the garden. He was supposed to draw the curtains when the sun reached the back of the house, but that made his pokey room feel even worse, like being locked up in a packing crate. Not 'his' room, exactly, Thelma had never called it that. She called it the 'guest room', though Seymour certainly didn't feel like a guest. People were supposed to be deferential to guests and make them feel welcome. Thelma had bestowed no such courtesy on him. She'd made it clear that his presence was inconvenient, even though he hadn't wanted to come and was bewildered by the whole arrangement. All he knew was that although he was supposed to spend three more weeks of the Christmas holidays with his dad, his mother had charged dramatically up to the caravan park and brought him home. Maybe she had a point – his father had made a boozy telephone call threatening to take Seymour away interstate for good. Seymour himself hadn't been particularly worried. His dad had made the same threat once or twice in the past, but as he rarely had the funds to travel even to the next town to find work, an interstate trip held as much likelihood as a visit to the moon. His mother, however, thrived on drama, no matter how shallow.

He glanced at his new watch, which his dad, coming home tipsily one night to the caravan park, had given him in a fit of maudlin remorse. Seymour hadn't wanted such a gift, but hadn't known a compassionate way to refuse it, either. And it wasn't really a gift, but more of a bribe for his permanent company.

It was only ten-thirty. Groaning with boredom and despair, he went up the hall and had another look through the coloured panels in the front door. All the houses in Victoria Road were exactly the same as Thelma's – single-fronted red brick, each with a miserly sliver of front garden and one window set beside the door. Those windows looked like a gallery of eyes watching him, saying,

'We see you, Seymour Kerley! Don't you dare step outside while Thelma's at work. She told you to stay inside, and we're here to make certain you do!' The whole street of one-eyed, spying houses was intimidating. Even their polished brass doorknobs looked like medals awarded for vigilance.

Seymour went back down the hall and out into the garden. His shirt clung damply to his armpits and his clay-coloured hair lay in plastered wisps across his forehead. He almost wished himself back in the caravan park, but that had been just as oppressive. His father, caught in a cycle of occasionally finding work, then being sacked for inefficiency, was not cheerful company. No place Seymour had ever lived in had been particularly pleasant as far as he could remember. He inspected the garden, hoping to relieve the tedium with some job that needed doing, but nothing was out of place, no hose to be coiled, not one weed growing amongst the sad hydrangeas.

He examined the gate, through which no one could possibly pass. It was as though Thelma believed that burglars prowled continually along the alleyway, just waiting for the chance to creep in and steal her tacky old TV set. The stiff, unused bolts couldn't even be moved in their brackets. He put his eye to the gap above the padlock, but could see only a stretch of bluestone flags with a central guttering, and the shabby corrugated iron fences of the back yards opposite. He placed one foot on the crossbar and scrambled up – a small, skinny, uncoordinated boy made timid by a lifetime of constant nagging. Eleven years of lectures clattered away in his mind now, as though someone had pressed a control button: 'Don't climb on things, Seymour, you'll rip your good shirt. Be careful, don't go near strange dogs, you never know if they'll bite. Did you remember to take your anti-histamine tablets? Don't do this, don't do that . . .'

The times in between, of staying with his dad, were in their own way just as restrictive. Uncertain, fluctuating moods had to be gauged and conversation trimmed accordingly, or you were likely to end up getting yelled at or sometimes hit. The blows, he knew, were never intended, but just rose from his father's chaotic despair. It wasn't just the job situation, either, Seymour reflected. Underneath all the blustering, his dad was scared stiff. He'd been labelled a no-hoper for so long, and that was his mother's doing, with her sharp accusing tongue. You didn't want someone bearing constant witness to your failure. Seymour could understand why a person would choose to drift and live apart. He could also understand why his dad so perversely clung to some remnant of family life – he was scared stiff of the uncertain future and loneliness. And that remnant happened to be Seymour himself. It was sad and depressing and he didn't know how he could handle things. Living with either of them, it was best to keep very quiet and not obtrude at all, and under the circumstances, he hadn't developed much expertise in climbing barriers or scaling any heights.

The forbidden alley looked sinister enough, thick with shadow, bordered by tall graffiti-scribbled fences. His knuckles ached from supporting himself at precarious chin height, so he drew his other foot up to the crossbar and stood at waist level, shutting his eyes quickly. His mother suffered from vertigo and kept her eyes shut even on escalators. She'd passed that phobia on to Seymour, or at least he'd always thought she had, but now to his surprise he discovered that this wasn't the case. He didn't feel giddiness when he opened his eyes and looked down from such a height, just relief as coolness from the flagstones wafted damply up into his face. The ground didn't swirl about below him; he didn't lose his balance and splatter his brains gorily all over the paving below.

He felt rather pleased with himself, and even defiant – a rare sensation for him. He glanced back over his shoulder at Thelma's unbearably smug little house, then craned forward to see what was at either end of the alleyway. There were two major roads, busy with passing traffic. He manoeuvred one leg right over the top of the gate, sat on the frame for a moment to gather his courage, then dropped down on to the flagstones. It was like escaping from a cage.

## CHAPTER TWO

SEYMOUR HEADED TOWARDS the main road at his left, keeping in the exact centre of the alleyway, fearful of many things. Any of the gates in the tall ribbed fencing on either side, for instance, could be flung open to disgorge sudden terrors – large dogs who wouldn't be calmed by the words of a peaceful stranger just passing through, or neighbours of Thelma (even though it was unlikely because she kept so much to herself) who might know that he wasn't supposed to leave the house in her absence. Worst of all, there could be kids his own age – brash, tough kids who would give him a hard time, as they always did, because he was fair game. He knew very well that he was fair game, but hadn't yet managed to figure out any defence mechanisms – only chameleon ones, which didn't always work. Breathing anxiously through his mouth, he kept his eyes fastened on the whirl of colour and movement at the left end of the alley and hurried towards it as fast as he could.

The main road down there was called Upton Street and its shops faced each other across a tram route.

Seymour had no money, but he walked along the nearest side carefully inspecting each shop in turn, as though he could buy anything he chose and had all day to think about it. There was a fruit shop, its counters piled high with golden oranges and soft dark grapes. Seymour looked at them with longing, swallowed hard and passed on. Next to it was a second-hand shop where he hesitated and then went in, because there were plenty of people in there and you could hide yourself easily enough in crowds. In a corner he found an old barber-shop chair, and added it to the private list of desirable things he'd one day have in his own room, if the situation of never quite knowing just where he'd be living ever resolved itself. He was always discovering things for that idealised room of his – cheerful bedspreads, desks with maps painted on them, carved teak chests. There was a chest in this particular shop, an old battered metal one with a rusty clasp. He knelt and tried to open the lid, visualising the whole thing enamelled in bright gloss with new brass hinges . . .

'Don't fiddle around with the lock, dear, unless you're planning to buy that trunk,' someone said, and although he hadn't really been doing anything, he shot up, red-faced, and retreated to the door, stumbling over his feet. Anyone who spoke to him with authority tended to have that effect. He scooted over the Victoria Road inter-section, then calmed down enough to stop and look into a sports-shop window at chrome and gleaming new leather. He pressed his palms sadly against the glass with pointless longing. How he'd love a new bike, not like that old battered second-hand thing which had been lost on one of their moves.

13

One time, before his mother had become so vindictive and bitter about such visits, he'd been staying with his father and came by a job cleaning out a butcher shop after school. He'd saved twenty-five dollars in a little tin box under his mattress. The flat box with embossed bells on the lid was treasure trove, found on a rubbish dump. The butcher's wife had told him that tins like that were used to send gift slices of wedding cake to guests who couldn't attend. So the tin with its pattern of bells had seemed fortunate, a symbol of perhaps managing to save enough money to buy a new bicycle. It hadn't fulfilled its promise, though. His dad had found the hidden money and spent it down at the pub.

After the sports shop there was a small wooden building with 'Upton Street Gospel Hall – I Am The Word' etched in flowery writing across a frosted glass window, and next to that a narrow park with palm trees and a sprinkler system maintaining a lawn. Seymour avoided the park – alarming, loud-voiced kids always hung around parks – and came to five adjoining shops under one long awning that made them look like a sliced log cake. They sold small multiple items – health food, baby clothes, wool, embroidery cottons. His mother was besotted with embroidery: 'fancywork' she called it – fussy little mats scattered with rosebuds and garlands. He had a fleeting, melancholy vision of his mum stitching away at her fancywork in the evenings. Heard her voice, carping monotonously about the troublesome life she'd had to lead ever since she'd become entangled with his father, the sacrifices she'd made. How she could barely afford that last dental bill, how his father never put himself out to get a proper job or hang on to one when he did, the promised maintenance payments that never arrived. Why, she could have married anyone! Given her time all over again, by now she could have a nice house and not have to work. Yes, she knew it was an old-fashioned viewpoint these days, but in her opinion women were happiest at full-time home-making. Only here she was in this miserable situation not of her own making, married to a no-good wastrel . . .

Seymour went very quickly past that particular shop window and came to a long stretch of ugly jerry-built flats riddled with little metal balconies. No one in their right mind would sit on balconies like that, he thought, even if there'd been room for a chair. Not unless they wanted to be asphyxiated by car fumes and deafened by traffic.

He crossed the street at the lights and began working his way back along the shops on the other side. There was a place where leadlight doors and windows were made, and a jovial man looked up and waved a soldering iron but Seymour moved on, too shy to wave back. An antique shop where a lady seated at a carved desk just inside the door gave him a hard, appraising stare when he peered in. A supermarket with howling toddlers and frazzled young mothers. An extension of the park which ran on this side also, cut in two by the busy main road.

The grass, dappled by leaf shadows, gave an irresistible illusion of coolness. He plucked at his long-sleeved shirt, which was made of cheap synthetic material. Thelma had bought it for him as he'd come to her house with so little clothing. Even with the sleeves rolled up, it was like being imprisoned inside a metal bin. He went into the park a little way and had a long drink from a bubbler, then wet his hanky. Thelma supplied him with a fussily ironed handkerchief each morning, not believing in tissues, which she said were a wicked waste of money. Seymour folded the wet hanky across his forehead, and as the park was empty, sat on a bench under a trellis. It was a mistake.

A bunch of rowdy kids, smug with assumed toughness, suddenly came racketing in from the shopping-centre entrance. They were shoving each other about and making a lot of noise with skateboards, but spotted Seymour at once. He got up nervously and tried to edge past to the safety of the main road, for he was a target, and they knew it as well as he did.

'Hey you, new kid round here, where'd ya score that shirt, off your grandpop?' someone sniggered.

Seymour didn't say anything. He pressed back against the bole of the tree, feeling the bark pattern imprint itself through his clothing, trying to make himself as secret as a lizard. But they didn't give up, they formed a closer semi-circle.

'Hey you, no spikka da English or something?'

Seymour kept his eyes on the ground, on the restless feet and little skateboard wheels. The wheels jiggled backwards and forwards, holding cached, impatient power, biding time. A hand darted out and grabbed at his handkerchief and someone yelled, 'Geeze, a snot rag! Maybe he's a little midget grandpa. Only grandpops carry hankies . . .'

He peeled himself away from the tree, plunged through an opening in the circle of feet, and scuttled back to the comparative safety of the shops. Glancing over his shoulder, he saw that the kids didn't intend to leave it at that. They'd followed, laughing and calling out after him, their day made. Heart thumping, he shot across the road with the green light, collecting a furious, 'Watch where you're going!' from a woman with a shopping jeep. His racing feet whisked him past blurred images of embroidery wool, health food, I Am The Word, chrome and leather, golden oranges, purple grapes – and blessedly to the alleyway opening. He dived into its dark tunnel, but didn't stop.

Corrugated fences flashed by, each looking exactly like the next, and in his bother he became hopelessly disorientated, couldn't remember which was Thelma's gate, even which side of the alley it was on. Those kids had spotted where he'd gone to ground. He didn't look back, but could hear them storm into the Upton Street end of the alleyway, baying insults and threats which could mean everything or nothing. He could hear the clatter of little nylon wheels across flagstones, and pounding feet. An empty aluminium drink can sailed past his ear and clanged against a gate post – maybe it was Thelma's gate post, but he couldn't even remember what colour that was.

There was a sudden unexpected break in the wall of iron on his left, a splash of light from a gate left ajar, and he darted in there and slammed the gate shut and stood against it, quaking. The feet stopped, the wheels stopped and someone rattled the gate half-heartedly and said, 'Aw, let's forget about that little wimp, for the time being, know what I mean? Probably nicked inside to tell his old lady on us. Come on, let's go down the oval.'

The feet stampeded past and there was just the muted,

innocuous rumble of main-street traffic. Nothing was new, nothing under the sun . . . confrontation and flight, huddling in some secret place trembling with cowardice. It happened inevitably at each new school, every new place he lived. All his strong resolutions made in lonely hours seemed doomed to come tumbling down like a flimsily built tower of plastic blocks. Seymour stood pressed against the gate for a long time.

17 Acacia Avenue
Merken

Dear Judith,

I'm sorry to trouble you, but I wondered if you have any idea where Angela is living now? She really is very inconsiderate about not letting us know when she moves, and some urgent mail (bills etc.) has turned up here for her.

Judith, I'm afraid my husband must have sounded very abrupt and rude when he arrived to collect her belongings from your flat last month. We were all very upset and things looked so hopeless and impossible. I do apologise for Stuart, he's been under a great deal of pressure and strain recently.

It was kind of you to put Angie up for those four days, especially when you're so cramped for space with the new baby. I'm sorry she abused your hospitality like that, it was unforgivable. She had no right to inconvenience you when she could easily have come out here to stay.

I've enclosed a stamped envelope in case you do know her new address and can let me know. We worry about her so much, this whole dreadful business seems like a nightmare. You've been such a good friend to her all this time, and I certainly don't blame you now for wanting to have nothing more to do with her after that scene at your flat.

If she does get in touch with you, would you please ask her to phone me immediately? I've tried all her other places and they don't know where she is. We're so terribly worried about her.

I was pleased to see how well you look, Judy. I hope the baby isn't causing you too many sleepless nights. She really is a little pet and so pretty. Judy, if you ever find things a strain, please don't hesitate to give me a ring or come out to visit. You seem to be coping marvellously, but I know how hard it can be with a young baby. You know, I often look back to when you and Angie were at school together, giggling over the phone to each other and trying out new hairstyles . . . oh dear, it seems only yesterday!

Take care, Judy, please let me know if I can help in any way, and please don't forget to pass my message on to Angie if she contacts you,

Love from Jeanette Easterbrook.

## CHAPTER THREE

'HELLO, WHERE DID YOU spring from, then?' someone said in a languid, just-woken-up voice and he saw that it belonged to a girl in her late teens, lying on a plastic couch in the sunshine. The voice held no belligerence, but he stared at her in alarm, not knowing how to explain that he'd sought refuge from a bunch of kids, some of them even younger than himself.

'I thought I'd shut that gate,' said the girl. 'But the catch on it keeps jerking open. Still, that's not my problem, is it? It's that old cow of a landlady who should do something about it. I haven't had anything nicked yet, but I guess there's always a first time. Was that what you had in mind, pal, sneaking in here to pinch stuff?'

'No! I just thought . . . thought it was my back gate,' Seymour lied, finding his voice at last. 'I just moved here and they all look the same from the alleyway.' His fingers scrabbled at the latch, seeking escape from this new predicament, but he found himself staring covertly at the girl. She was the most beautiful person he'd ever seen in his life. Her large gentle eyes were the colour of rain-wet lichen, fringed with dark lashes that curled back upon themselves, and although she was a grown-up, she wasn't really threatening in any way. She just lay there soaking up the sun, quiet and calm and easy-going, with her hands linked behind her head.

'Don't take off, I won't bite you,' she said. 'What's your name?'

'S . . . Seymour.' The embarrassment of saying aloud that pretentious name, which sat so uneasily upon him! It should, he thought, belong to a middle-aged business man with a grey suit and briefcase.

'That's nice,' said the girl. 'Sort of classy. My name's Angela, but you can call me Angie if you like.'

Her long hair, haloed by the sun, seemed composed of fine gold and silvery threads. Angela, Angie, Angel . . .

'Listen, Seymour, would you like to be a real pal and make me a cup of coffee?' the angel said lazily. 'You'll find everything just inside that door there, even though it looks like a barn, but it's not, it's my flat. Sixty-five dollars a week and don't you reckon that's a rip-off for a shed in a back yard? I ought to report her to the Tenants' Union, still . . . what was I saying, oh yeah, you'll find cups and stuff next to the sink, but don't take any notice of the mess, okay? I haven't got around to cleaning things up today yet. Make a cuppa for yourself, too, why don't you? Oh, and would you mind emptying this ashtray while you're in there? There should be a plastic bin next to the sink.'

She started taking polish remover and cotton wool out of a little pink basket and began to manicure her nails. Not knowing how to refuse, Seymour edged past reluctantly and up two shallow steps into an extremely messy room. The far end contained a hideous old wardrobe with a mottled mirror set in its door and an unmade bed strewn with clothes. In the nearer section was an ancient gas stove, a jumble of tiny cupboards and a sink. It was difficult to find cups amongst all the junk, hard to find anything.

He filled an electric jug and switched it on to boil, dug two chipped mugs out of the pile in the sink and washed them, found a jar of instant coffee, and sugar congealed in a blue pottery bowl without a lid. There was a small fridge in a corner, containing only a few cans of beer, chocolate yoghurt and a carton of dubious milk. He put everything neatly on a tray and carried it back outside.

'You're a real star! Not many people can make a good cuppa, but you're certainly one of them!' Angie said, sounding so warm and grateful that Seymour blushed, unused to praise of any description. 'Don't stand up to drink it, grab a cushion and sit down and make yourself at home. Talk to me. If there's one thing I love, it's having someone to chat to while I'm doing my nails. Though you're not exactly chatty, are you? Never mind, you can just sit there and listen and I'll do all the earbashing. I'm pretty good at it, they tell me.'

Seymour perched self-consciously on the lowest step leading up to the flat – if you could call it a proper flat. He sipped the coffee, trying not to think of the mess in the kitchen. You couldn't be brought up by people like his mother and Thelma without being fastidious, but he was too polite to show reluctance at having to drink from a cup that had been in such a grotty sink. It was strange, really, because the girl herself was so immaculate, her hair sparkling like water in the sun.

He watched, fascinated, as she attended to her nails. They were long and perfectly shaped and she was obviously very proud of them, spreading her hands out like a temple dancer. She shaped each nail with a slim pearl-handled file, then began to apply the lacquer. Jet black. Seymour had never seen anyone wearing black nail varnish before. Her clothes were unusual, too. She was wearing a short satin skirt and a blouse like a singlet, only made rather startlingly from silver lace. She bent to pick up a dropped pair of manicure scissors and Seymour nearly dropped his coffee mug. There was a tattoo – a little blue horse with outspread wings, stencilled on one shoulder. He'd never known anyone with a tattoo before, specially not a girl.

'Hey, how about I paint your nails for you?' she teased, and he shook his head vehemently. 'Go on, live dangerously. Think of the sensation you'd cause.'

'No! I mean, no thanks. Thelma . . . the lady I stay with, she'd go bananas if I came home wearing black nail polish! Geeze, blokes don't wear nail polish!'

'Go on, is that so?' Angie said, smirking. 'Well, never mind, one day I'll sneak up on you when you're asleep and paint your nails, toes and all. Cut your hair, too, while I'm about it, and make you . . . well, let's say different. So, I guess you're on school holidays, are you?'

He nodded soberly, thinking of the excruciating four weeks before him, all those barren days like a long dusty road leading to nowhere in particular. 'I've got nothing to do,' he said. 'I reckon I'll be glad when school starts again.'

'You're crazy. Holidays are lovely! I'm on one, too, sort of,' Angie said. 'Well, between jobs, at any rate. What I'm really planning to do is open my own florist shop. Bet you never guessed I was a qualified florist, did you? Well, I am. At least, I never actually got the certificate yet, but near enough as makes no difference.'

Seymour felt impressed. She didn't seem quite old enough to be the potential owner of a shop, but she was so unusual, so unlike anyone else, that the idea didn't seem very outlandish. Anyone who wore satin and silver lace and black nail polish, anyone who had a little flying horse tattooed on one shoulder, could reach heights undreamed of by other people.

'I've got a name already picked out for my shop,' Angie boasted. ' "Fleur". That's French for flower. Cute, isn't it? And I'm going to have the benches and walls and floor and everything snowy white to set off all the flower arrangements, and a ceiling made out of that opalescent stuff you see inside shells on the beach. What do you think about that? I'm going to specialise in bridal bouquets, too, that's where the big money is.'

Seymour was captivated, having no difficulty in imagining such a shop, with Angie at its fragrant centre. He pictured himself inside the shop with her, permitted to watch as she arranged soft boughs of blossom, being allowed to make morning coffee in opalescent mugs, getting praised for it . . .

'Have to get some money saved up first, though,' Angie said and sighed and tossed all the manicure tools back into the little basket. 'Bring the mugs inside, will you, Seymour? The old dragon nearly has a hernia if you even leave a clothes peg on the ground out here.'

She seemed quite proud of her flat, despite the horrendous mess. 'Completely self-contained,' she bragged, pulling back a curtain to display a tiny bathroom. 'I've hardly ever managed to get a self-contained place before, you know, rents are that high. It's been . . . well, sharing flats with real no-hopers, and sleazy old boarding houses where you could pick up God knows what from standing on the bath mat. This is only temporary, though. My boyfriend, when he gets . . . well, pretty soon he'll be in a position to put down the deposit on our own proper house. I don't know where yet, maybe a little place in the country. You could come and visit us, even though you never open your mouth to say more than two words strung together. Jas and me, we'll keep chooks and grow all our own vegies and get an Old English Sheepdog and we'll have a duck pond. I'm loopy about ducks. I used to have this fantastic pottery duck collection, only someone's nicked it or I've lost it or something, I can't remember exactly . . . Oh, strewth . . . it can't be, is that the time? Someone's pinched the whole morning off me! I'd better get my skates on now.'

Seymour said hastily, 'Thanks for the coffee. And I'm sorry, I didn't mean to hold you up.' He was so accustomed to things being deemed his fault that the apology tumbled out as automatically as breathing.

'I held myself up, and you don't have to go,' Angie said, surprised. 'Hang around a bit. You're a nice polite kid, not loud mouthed and sassy like those other little yobs who live round here. And I didn't mean it about you being too quiet. I kind of like it, because I natter on so much. Tell you what, while I have a quick shower, why don't you pick out some earrings for me to wear? They're all in this box.'

While she was singing blithely in the shower, he tipped the collection of earrings on to the bedspread and sorted them into pairs. There were dozens of them – shells, moulded flowers, feathers, little animal shapes, silver dragonflies, swathes of sparkling multi-coloured stones. Using a couple of pink tissues from the box on Angie's dressing-table, he lined the jewellery case and arranged all the paired earrings inside. The dressing-table wasn't a proper one, just a small battered table with a propped-up mirror. Its surface was cluttered with cosmetics, cheap ornaments and magazines, and looked as though it hadn't been tidied in weeks. Thelma, he thought, wouldn't have tidied it, she would have dumped the whole lot straight into a rubbish bin.

Angie came out of the shower and twirled about showing off a change of clothing. She was dressed completely in pink: a ruffled dress tied in narrow pink ribbons over her shoulders, pink plastic bangles that jangled from wrist to elbow, a long rose-coloured scarf knotted about her head with the fringed ends falling down one side of her face. She looked, to Seymour, as fresh and pretty as a carnation.

'Well, now, what do you think?' she said seriously. 'Your honest opinion, mind, not just being smarmy. Are these shoes all right, or do you think I should wear my white sandals?'

'I kind of like those shiny ones you've got on already,' he said, unaccustomed to being called upon to give advice about girls' clothes. He held out the earrings he'd chosen, tiny pink roses, because Angie had been so radiant when talking about her florist shop.

'Thanks, love, you picked out a really good pair to go with Susan-Jane. I couldn't have done better myself.'

'Susan-Jane?'

'That's the name of this dress. I give all my clothes names, like this one's sort of little girly and frilly, so Susan-Jane suits it, don't you reckon?' Angie held her long hair back to put the roses in, and he saw that she already had several silver hoops and studs in each ear lobe.

She sprayed herself lavishly with perfume, pretended to do the same to him and followed, giggling, as he retreated outside.

'Very funny!' Seymour said.

'Well, your expression certainly was – you just should have seen your face! Now then, where's my blasted key . . . must be my lucky day, here it is right on top of the junk in my bag, and not only that, my spare key, too! Thought I'd lost both of them. I'm always losing stuff and locking myself out, so I had this other one cut.'

'It's pretty mad, carrying them both together,' Seymour said, still upset about the perfume. 'Most people leave their spare key under a flowerpot or something, for an emergency.'

'Quite right, too, professor,' Angie said and danced across the paved yard, holding out the wide ruffled skirt of her dress. She slipped the spare key under a flowerpot, then held the gate open and motioned him through. 'Off you go now. Scoot! Might see you around some time, chatterbox.'

Seymour looked out at the alleyway and remembered

those terrifying kids who were perhaps still lurking there like Ninjas. Waiting for him to reappear. What they'd said about going to the oval, that could have been a ruse. He'd been tricked like that before. He hovered by the steps, unable to move, gazing at Angela with scared eyes.

'Hey, what's up?'

'I don't . . . don't . . . know which is my back gate,' Seymour managed to get out. 'Didn't I tell you? I'm staying with this lady, Thelma . . . she's a friend of my mum's, sort of . . . and I climbed over her back gate and went up the shops and now I'm . . . lost. The house number's 37 Victoria Road, but I can't go around that way. Got no front door key, and there's a trellis thing on the side path and it's kept locked. I don't know what to do . . .'

'Well, don't panic. You've struck it lucky, because I just happen to be going out that way. As a matter of fact I always do, so my landlady can't bail me up and have a moaning session. Come on, then, useless. You'd be dead hopeless if you were one of those guys they sent off to explore the moon, you'd probably have landed up on Mars instead. Can't even find your own back gate, I don't know! Now, Victoria Road's over that side, so your gate must be along here somewhere. The toffy-nose side of the alley, if it's even got one.'

Seymour looked anxiously up and down the alley, but it was deserted. Almost immediately he recognised Thelma's gate, directly opposite, with the crescent-shaped cut above the lock. He climbed up with no difficulty, then sat on the top rail and looked down at Angela, thinking that in that setting of garbage bins and ugly corrugated iron, she was like a waterlily floating on a murky pond surface. But now she was turning to go, and he'd probably never see her again, and she was the only person he'd ever met in his life who'd made him feel as though his company was remarkable or worthwhile.

'Hey, Angie . . .'

She turned back and looked at him enquiringly, but he had nothing else to say. He just sat and gazed down at her from the loneliest face in the world.

'Okay,' she said. 'Bored, aren't you, nothing to do in the holidays. Well, listen, I just thought, how about you turn up at my place tomorrow around ten-thirty? I've got to go someplace first, but soon as we get that out of the way, I'll take you on a tram ride and show you something really fantastic. It can be a special holiday treat.'

'You mean it?' he asked breathlessly, hardly daring to believe it could be so.

'Course I mean it!' said Angela.

## BUDGET

**Rent**   $65 (what a rip off!)
**Elect a/c**   $47 (apply for extension of time if poss?)
**D.M.**   $450 (!!!)
**Rick**   $76 (?) LIAR!!
**Part payment on black dress**   $5
**Floral art course outstanding fees**   final notice hell
damn and blast!   $100 less deposit = $75


### NEEDED URGENTLY:
milk    coffee    groceries/fruit    pantyhose
hair colour rinse    detergent powder    Ant-Rid
bulb for kitchen light    new jeans


In savings a/c   $11.50
In Jas's a/c   ? (Mustn't touch!)
Dole cheque due Tues
Sickness benefit? Wangle it somehow? Through Rick
or Gayle maybe?

Loan from Jude $15 (pay back out of dole cheque)
Sell leather jacket to Recycle Shop? How much?
In handbag   $7.57 (!!!!!!!!!!!)

**HARD TIMES !!!!!!!!!!!!!**

## CHAPTER FOUR

'I'LL BE ABLE TO TELL YOUR mum when she comes on Friday you've been a good obedient boy and given no trouble,' Thelma said. 'Or hardly any.'

He knew that meant the small scorch mark on the kitchen table where he'd absent-mindedly put down the hot saucepan last night. Thelma had been referring to it obliquely ever since.

'With all this extra time you've got for study, you might even be ahead of the others in your class when you go back to school,' she said. 'If you look at it like that, it makes up for not being able to roam about on your own for a week or so. Not that that's important. We all have our crosses to bear in this world, every one of us. You can't start too early in life to learn what's in store and people make a big mistake thinking everything should be fun. Now, Seymour, today you can make do with a couple of boiled eggs for lunch. Put bicarb soda in that little aluminium saucepan to soak afterwards, so it doesn't discolour, and I'll be home by six.'

At last she was gone, clomping away down the street in her sensible shoes, and Seymour put the chain back on the door. He waited alone in the quiet house, listening to the mantel clock ticking imperiously from the front room and the heat crackling on the roof. At ten-thirty precisely he crossed the alley and went in through Angie's gate.

No one answered his knock on the door. He'd thought himself immune to disappointment, and wasn't prepared for the sense of loss that assailed him now, of something promised and denied. He knocked several times more, quiet, tentative, despairing little knocks, and finally tried the handle, to discover that Angie must have gone out and left the door unlocked. It swung lightly inwards, catching against her striped handbag lying on the floor. There was one pink satin shoe tossed carelessly on a chair with plastic bangles on top.

'Angie? Angela, you still here?' he called in a voice as insubstantial as the movement of a leaf. He hesitated on the step. Women never went out anywhere without their handbags, he thought, hopes rising. Angela might have just gone into the main house for a minute, to see her landlady about something. Surely she couldn't have forgotten that invitation of yesterday!

Uncertainly, he went in and picked up the fallen mate to the shoe, paired them neatly on the chair, and then spun around as a drowsy voice, fluttering from the edge of sleep, murmured from the bed, 'Who's that? Is it you, Jas? I never . . . I couldn't find . . . Oh my God, it was so cold, it was so dark . . .'

She sat up in her tumbled bed and gazed at Seymour for a moment as though she'd never seen him before in her life. Then she picked up the alarm clock, shook it disbelievingly and wailed, 'Oh hell, the bloody thing didn't go off! Or else I forgot to set it or something dumb . . . now I'm going to be late! Be a love and make us a cup of strong black coffee, plenty of sugar, would you?'

While she was in the shower he washed out yesterday's cups and set the tray, transferring some of the sugar to a fairly clean glass bowl. There was a shrub just by the steps, bearing a few determined pallid flowers. Impulsively he reached out and broke off a sprig and set it on the tray next to Angie's cup. She emerged from the shower and sat at the makeshift dressing-table to comb her hair. Watching her reflection, Seymour thought that each tug of the comb seemed to cause her pain and that she also looked pale, almost waxen, like the flowers. When she noticed the spray he thought she was about to cry. But then the corners of her mouth tilted upwards into a sparkling smile.

'Why, mate, that's terrific! That's really sweet, putting flowers on the tray, you make me feel special. No kidding, I always know straight off if I'm going to hit it off with people, and I wasn't wrong about you, was I?'

Seymour sat, dazzled with happiness. Once, he remembered, he'd bought a bunch of early violets for his mother. She'd said, 'It's rather a waste of money, violets don't last much longer than one day. Didn't you know that, Seymour?' Angie put on her make-up and when she'd finished, she picked up the flower spray and tucked it behind her ear. He stopped thinking about those other flowers, the violets.

'Angie, if you don't feel well, you don't have to worry

34

about going out,' he said generously, still concerned about her pallor.

'But I feel okay,' she said, surprised. 'Why shouldn't I be? I'm always a bit slow and dithery first thing in the morning, that's all, but once I've had my coffee I'm ready to take on the whole world. You wait and see.'

'Coffee's not enough for your breakfast,' he said awkwardly, trying not to sound like Thelma. 'You should eat something to go with it.'

'Well, I never feel hungry till round about lunch time. Not even then, sometimes. Probably got a different metal . . . metab . . .'

'Metabolism?'

'Yeah, that's the word. I've just got a different metabolism to everyone else. Maybe I was supposed to be born on another planet and got landed here by mistake. Saturn, that's the one I'd choose, that one with all the gorgeous spinning rings. Seymour, does this outfit look okay? Do I look smashing?'

It was as though she really cared about his opinion and, flattered, he nodded, though Angie really looked more suitably dressed for a party than a midday tram ride. She was wearing a dress that was sometimes blue and sometimes pearl green, and looking at it more closely, he saw that the material was textured in scalloped patterns which made the colours shimmer into each other. She also wore high-heeled silver sandals, and he decided that although it wasn't the sort of thing people wore in the day time, it somehow looked just right on Angie, who was so beautiful.

'Neptunia,' she said. 'That's what I call this dress,

because it looks like under the sea. Chosen my earrings yet? You did such a good job last time, I'll let you be my official earring selector.'

He opened the box and found a pair of large iridescent hoops to go with Neptunia.

'Oh, I just adore summer!' Angie carolled when they went out through the back gate into the alleyway. 'What I'm going to do one of these days is nick off to Queensland and open a little craft shop. I'm pretty good at making things, you know, handcrafts and that. I got A's right through school for art. If only I could get some money together, I could easily run a little craft shop and sell all the stuff I make. Shell necklaces and straw sun hats and umbrellas with flowers painted on them, things like that. But at lunch times I'd shut up that shop and just lie on the beach all afternoon. What a life, eh? How about if you came with me to Queensland? You could do with a suntan. Your folks probably wouldn't even notice you'd gone, either, you're that quiet.'

Seymour, conscious of the length of the alleyway to the main road, of all its possible dangers, was too preoccupied to answer. He kept close to her side, even though no one else was about in the warm, still morning. Angela walked carelessly, as though the alley were a peaceful country lane, stopping to pat a stray cat, standing on tiptoe to look over a fence at a hanging basket of fern.

'I'm dead crazy about plants,' she said. 'Always buying them down at the market, though they usually curl up their little toes and die on me. I sort of forget to water them. I used to have this really cute one, it was called . . . oh, chain of hearts, something like that. It had long strings that dangled down and all these darling silvery green heart leaves growing on them. Plants are like people. You can talk to them and get energy from them, did you know that? And someone at a university or somewhere brainy carried out these tests and found out they react to music and to fights going on. They're sensitive. It's like they're crying if people have a fight in the same room.'

Seymour hadn't known any of that. His mother disliked house plants and Thelma had only one, a rubbery dark thing in the living room with sharp leaves like accusingly pointed hands. He knew all about quarrels taking place in rooms, though, but put that firmly out of his mind.

'Where is it we're going, Angie?' he asked at the tram stop.

Angela looked at him blankly. 'Oh, are you catching the tram, then?' she said. 'I didn't realise. I thought you were just being a gent, walking me up to the corner.'

'Yesterday . . .' Seymour said. 'You know, you said to come by and we'd go on the tram and you'd show me this terrific place you know about.'

'Did I?'

She sounded genuinely puzzled, and in his embarrassment, Seymour began to apologise, not even knowing what he was apologising for. 'I'm sorry. It's just . . . you said. I must have got it wrong. Never mind, though, it doesn't matter. I'll just . . .' He'd have to face the return trip up the alley all by himself, face all the dangers. Back to that bleak little house, where maybe he'd tackle some of the neglected school work, and perhaps sleep for a couple of hours. That would demolish at least part of the long day.

'Hey, kid, don't go nicking off on me!' Angie called after him. 'I just forgot for a minute, that's all. My memory's like a leaky old sieve, I'm always getting into strife for it. You can still come with me. I reckon it's a great idea, we'll have an absolutely fantastic time. Only thing is, I've got to go somewhere else first, and it's a long boring bus ride, all the way out to North Road terminal, last stop on the route. But once that's over I'm not doing anything special. Oh, I do remember now, yesterday, and what I said I was going to show you!'

'What is it?' he demanded, brimming with renewed happiness.

'Never you mind,' Angie said mysteriously. 'It won't be a surprise if I tell you beforehand, will it? Got any money on you to help out with the fares? I'm a bit . . . well, sort of short this week. I had an account I had to pay up or else.'

Abjectly he drew out the sixty cents which was all he'd managed to scrape together, going through every pocket he owned. It was in small pieces, mostly copper, and he looked at it sadly, wishing it were a hundred times that amount. So that he could not only pay for both their fares, but lunch, too, and maybe buy her a chain-of-hearts plant, if they just happened to pass a plant nursery.

'Last of the big spenders, eh?' Angie said. 'Oh well, we'll manage somehow.'

People glanced at her as they boarded the bus and the glances turned into open staring. Seymour stood a little taller, proud to be seen with such a spectacular grown-up girl. He hoped that some of her glory was spilling over upon him, that they'd all think she was related to him, his big sister, maybe, or a very young aunt. He knew without a doubt that she was the most glamorous person on that whole bus and probably in the whole world. She paid Seymour's fare, then flashed both an enchanting smile and a little perspex card at the driver and said 'Student concession' when paying her own fare.

'Student concession? Don't you have to be at university or a college or something for that?' he asked when they found seats up at the back and she'd put the card away in her handbag. 'I thought you said you . . .'

'Look at those boats on the river, Seymour!' she interrupted. 'Wow, don't those guys all think they're Superman! Though it's not all that marvellous, that crew rowing stuff. Jas, that's my boyfriend I told you about, he knows how to shoot rapids in a canoe and things like you see on telly. He was into martial arts, too, got as far as brown belt. You name it – boxing, rock climbing, Jas can do all of those things!'

Seymour contemplated the magnificence of knowing how to guide a craft through snags and rocks, of being trained in martial arts, of scaling cliff faces. Maybe Jas would just happen to drop in to visit Angie when he was there, and offer to teach him a couple of basic karate punches or kicks or something. Then he could walk the whole length of the alley any time he liked without his heart threatening to burst from fear. Would it be too pushy to ask Angie if she could introduce him to her boyfriend? He turned towards her, but her head was on the seat backrest and her eyes closed. Resting lightly on the bag, her folded hands were as gentle as sleeping doves, but each time the bus jolted to a stop, her thumbs jerked inwards towards the palms, making small tense fists. It was hard to tell if she were asleep or not, but he didn't disturb her.

If it were sleep, she seemed to possess an inbuilt reaction to distance and correct bus stops. When they reached the terminal and the bus made a U-turn, her eyes snapped open immediately. She leaped up and pulled him out after her, shoving past startled passengers. She hurried him through a small shopping centre and turned into a long straight highway busy with lumbering trucks and vans. It was an ugly road, lined on either side by raw-looking factories and vacant blocks of land.

'Come on, pal, don't dawdle!' she said rather testily, though he was doing his best to keep up. 'We've got a long walk ahead of us. There's supposed to be a connecting bus route along here, but the damned thing only runs about every two hours, so walking's quicker in the long run. All this used to be market gardens and orchards once. Isn't it a pity how they always go and muck nice things up? We used to drive down here to get to the beach at weekends. It was great.'

'Who's we? You mean Jas and you?'

'No, this was when I was a kid. My parents and my brother and sister. See where that car yard is, there used to be a cute little house. You should have seen it, it had a weathervane on the roof and ivy round the windows. I always reckoned I'd buy that cottage and live in it when I grew up, but they went and pulled it down, the rotten . . . oops, language, I'd better set you a good example, hadn't I? There was this pretty statue in the middle of the lawn, a lady holding a . . . oh, what do you call them, those things they played in ancient Rome . . .'

'A lyre?'

'Yeah, something like that. You never saw anything as nice as that old statue, though my sister reckoned it was tizzy. I used to call it Andromeda, but she changed it to Narelle.'

Nothing about the long road was nice now. There was no footpath so they walked on the gravelled verge, conversation becoming impossible because of a convoy of passing trucks. Angie's pace quickened even more in spite of the gravel and her high heels, and Seymour wondered why she was walking so fast, so urgently, but he didn't like to seem nosey by asking questions. She glanced at her watch as they completed a long uphill stretch and turned into an asphalted driveway with a sign saying 'Ambulances Only'.

'It's kind of a weird place to have a hospital, isn't it, stuck out here away from everything?' Seymour said. 'Are you visiting someone who's sick in there, Angie?'

'No, nothing like that. I've just got to pick up something, some medicine I've got to take every day. Waste of time, really, can't say it's doing anything to . . . Well, anyway, I'll only be a minute. Hospitals aren't all that fascinating, so you don't have to come in with me. Just wait out here on the lawn, okay? There's goldfish in that little pond you can look at, only don't be a dag and fall in. I'll be back in a couple of shakes, promise.'

He sat down on the concrete rim of the pool while Angie went up a ramp into a low red-brick building. It didn't look like an ordinary hospital, he thought idly. Once he'd stayed with his father in a motel opposite a hospital and they'd had to keep the windows shut to block out the constant noise of traffic and people. But this place was very quiet, hushed almost, and the only people about were a few men sitting in cane chairs at one end of an open veranda. They didn't take any notice of him. They just sat huddled into their own thoughts, not even chatting to one another. At first he thought they were elderly people. It was the way they sat, as though laden with the cares and loneliness of old age, but when he glanced at them properly, blinking against the raw sunlight, he saw that some of them were quite young men. He looked away and down into the pool at the goldfish instead, but almost immediately, Angela came back. She was walking normally, not in any particular hurry now, and appeared to be rather pleased with herself.

'Well, I won that round!' she said. 'They weren't going to let me have it just because I was ten minutes late.'

'Why can't you get your medicine from a chemist, like on a doctor's prescription? Thelma's got to take stuff for arthritis, but she just . . .'

'Well, my medicine's sort of different. It's like when you've got to go to a specialist for something instead of an ordinary doc. Believe you me, if there was any other way, I wouldn't be hiking out to this dump every day! Geeze, I hate that Marilyn! She's the boss lady in there and does she chuck her weight around, but no worries, she backed off this time. A lousy ten minutes late . . . the fuss she made! Know what I told her? I told her I couldn't help being late seeing I had to pick up my little brother because it's school holidays and I'm taking him out for the day. So, Seymour, little brother, let's go and have some fun!'

Dear Dr Tyburn,

I guess I'd better say thanks for getting me on the North Road program. I should have said it in the surgery instead of ranting and raving and carrying on. Sorry, I didn't mean to. I was just feeling pretty low and miserable.

Listen, would you do me a favour and not mention Nth. Rd to Dad if you see him at golf or anywhere around? I haven't told them at home. They'll only get their hopes up all over again. Maybe for nothing.

I did what you said and went out to see Marilyn and fix up about times etc. I appreciate how you got my name put ahead on that waiting list, but I don't know, doc. I'm sick to death of things. I was feeling so browned off I really was going to nick of to W.A. and start all over again where no one knows me, but like you said it would only be running away and taking the whole mess with me.

Wish I could be more positive about North Road. It's not going to work, you know! It never worked for anyone else I know, only Judy. But OK, I'll give it a try.


Angie.


P.S. You always were my favourite doc at Merken Clinic.

P.P.S. Remember that time when I was six and had to have a tetanus booster and you told me I was allowed to say one really bad word under

my breath if it hurt? Well, talk about
laugh – you know what I said? FUNGUS. (I
used to think that was a really heavy swear
word!)
P.P.P.S. Having to go on that fungus program!
It's OK, don't get your stethoscope in a knot,
I'm not backing out, I'll show up, damn it!
(Fungus fungus fungus!!!)

## CHAPTER FIVE

'ISN'T IT JUST FANTASTIC?' she said. 'You can have any mansion you fancy, only don't you dare go picking number seventeen. I've got my own eye on that one.'

Gresham Avenue: it could have been called Paradise, Seymour thought, as they walked slowly up one pavement and down the other. The houses were like great white ocean liners berthed in calm harbours. Decorative gates guarded wide sweeping lawns, stately roofs soared to the sky, and the whole avenue was fragrant with perfume.

'Roses, roses, all the way,' Angie said. 'They can all afford full-time gardeners here on Nobs' Hill. How about this one for you, Seymour? If I lived in number seventeen, we could wave across the street to each other in the mornings.'

Seymour gazed up at the tall, elegant house and tried to imagine himself looking down from the diamond-paned window and waving to Angela in number seventeen. But the house was too grand. He didn't know anyone who lived in a house like that, and couldn't visualise himself in it. Angie had no such trouble.

'Definitely number seventeen for me,' she said dreamily. 'Jas is going to buy it for me, soon as he gets out . . . soon as he gets himself fixed up with a job. We found this street by accident. We were at this great party in Ricky's flat the other side of the tram track – wow, some party that was! Coming home we took a short cut, only we got lost and found all these white walls shining in the moonlight. I often come out here and walk up and down and drool. I knew you'd like it, too.'

'Are you and Jas really going to buy number seventeen and live there?'

'Sure we are. One day it'll come up for auction and we'll be there with a big fat cheque in our hot little hands. It's going to be convenient, too, because there's a shopping centre just around the corner, and that's where I'll set up my florist shop. A florist shop in a posh area like this, you'd make a mint! And just wait till you see the shops, they're absolutely unreal, too!'

The shopping complex wasn't a slick modern one with escalators and malls, but two terraced rows facing each other graciously across a garden courtyard. It was too posh, Seymour thought, too aware of its own importance. He felt ill at ease, but Angie, full of aplomb, stopped to inspect a dress in a window.

'Well, I can't say I fancy that much,' she said critically. 'It's a nothing sort of colour, like smoke. I usually go for pretty colours, you know, bright and happy, or glittery things. I just love things that sparkle. That one probably costs hundreds of dollars, though you notice it hasn't even got a price tag. Price tags would be too vulgar for round here, I guess. That dress is too long, too. If you've got good legs, you shouldn't be ashamed to show them off. I reckon I've got good legs, don't you?'

Seymour felt embarrassed, but because she plainly expected an opinion from him, he nodded. He thought she must have good legs, the way people turned around to look at her. Again, he couldn't help noticing how they all did that, even though they pretended not to be staring, but Angie seemed sunnily unaware of it. Glamorous people, he supposed, must become used to people turning their heads to look, even bored by it.

'Let's go and check out that gift shop,' Angie said. 'I've got to get my mum a birthday present and you can help me choose it. It was her birthday last month, but I was . . . Well, it's a long story, but the fact is I never got around to buying her a present. So I want to get something really special now to make up.'

The gift shop was lined with glass shelves holding splendid things – china platters, carved wooden fruit, crystals, embossed-leather writing folders and boxes of wonderful stationery. There was a small long-stemmed rose, intricately fashioned from gold metal, complete with gold thorns and leaves and a dewdrop resting on one petal. It lay all by itself on a coral velvet board.

'There you are, Angie!' Seymour said. 'Why don't you get that for your mum? It's just right, you being a florist.'

'That rose? Yes, it's gorgeous . . . but hang on, look what it says on the price label, for heaven's sake!'

A shop assistant came over to them, wanting to know if they required help. 'May I show you anything in particular?' she said austerely, and Seymour could sense her eyes flicking at him briefly, but nonetheless taking in every detail of his shabby jeans, his cheap sandals and shirt, then dismissing him altogether and switching attention to Angela, eyes narrowed. Jealous, Seymour thought defensively. She's just dead jealous of Angie being so pretty and wearing clothes no one else has.

'We're just looking,' Angie said, apparently not at all bothered by such scrutiny. She knelt to rummage about in a basket of soap, picking one up and sniffing it appreciatively, then handing it to Seymour.

'Please don't touch the displays,' the assistant said.

'But how am I supposed to know if I like the smell or not?' Angie said. 'We're not hurting anything. How could you possibly damage a cake of soap just touching it?'

'That's not the point. The sign up there says not to handle the items on display. They've all been carefully arranged.'

'Oh, pardon me, I'm most terribly sorry,' Angie said contritely, but with sarcasm spiking her voice. She moved on with exaggerated care to look at a shelf of pot-pourri containers. The assistant hovered, almost as though daring her to touch another thing, but Angie just minced sedately along the shelf, with her hands linked behind her back. Her eyes were wide and innocent and her lower lip tucked behind her teeth. It was as though she were miming the role of a good obedient child, but the overall impression was one of impudence.

'Angie, how about we go and grab something to eat, a sandwich or something?' Seymour whispered uneasily. 'And you could buy your mum a pot plant instead. They have them at that market near Victoria Road, don't they? It's all too dear, this stuff.'

'I haven't finished looking yet, even though they think we're not good enough for their old shop,' Angie said, not troubling to lower her voice.

'If we haven't anything to suit you, I suggest you try elsewhere,' the assistant said coldly, and turned to attend to other customers who'd just come in.

Seymour, crimson, tugged Angie towards the door. She took her time getting there, dropping her bag halfway and shaking him off when he bent to help her pick up her scattered possessions. Almost through the door, she stopped and called, 'Hey, Miss!' The assistant frowned at her in exasperation. 'Your bra strap's showing, did you know? Wow, some bra, looks like a parachute harness!' Angie said, stuck her tongue out, then grabbed Seymour's hand and hurried him back through the courtyard. 'Did you see her face?' she gloated. 'Serves the sour old thing right, the way she was looking down her nose at us! You just wait, one day I'm going to set up my florist shop right next door to her crappy old place, and I'll have a whole section stocked with gifts much better than hers, and put her right out of business!'

'Angie, honest, you shouldn't have given her cheek like that!' Seymour said, being bundled on to a tram with no explanation. 'And where are we off to now? This goes back into town, doesn't it?'

'Sure does, and I'm going to shout you lunch at McDonald's.'

Angie settled back on the tram seat, smiling secretively to herself and apparently unrepentant about being rude to the shop assistant. She took out a nail file and began to smooth her nails.

Seymour looked back for one last glimpse of the

**49**

splendid mansions in Gresham Avenue. There was no harm in dreaming. Maybe one day he'd live in the one with diamond windows and Angela would live at number seventeen and they'd wave to each other each morning. Perhaps she'd let him work in her florist shop when he was old enough, too. You'd have to buy flowers fresh from the market early each morning, and he could do that job. He'd have a smart little van with the shop's name written on the side. It would be peaceful and undemanding, a job like that, the type of thing he could easily handle. He knew he wasn't particularly bright at school and couldn't expect much in the way of a career, but a job like that, just to start off with . . .

He even thought of asking Angie now to keep him in mind for it in a few years time, but when he turned to her, she was dozing. The nail file was slipping from her fingers. She was like a cat, he thought indulgently, suddenly yawning her head off like that and taking a little nap in public. Asleep in that manner, she didn't look grown up at all, but vulnerable, almost like a small child slumbering in a pram in a department store. Her dress changed colour as the tram rocked from stop to stop, like shells altering colour under water, and her head nodded and finally slid down to rest on his shoulder. Her bag was in danger of tumbling to the floor. He grabbed it just in time and put the nail file back inside. And saw, nestled amongst the contents, the gold rose from the gift shop.

He sat very still, peering gravely at the metal rose, and thought, 'Of course she paid for it, must have been while I was putting the soap back . . . Only – why was that assistant so snooty to her after she bought something

as expensive as that? Of course she paid for it! ...
Only – why didn't they wrap it up for her? In posh shops
like that, they always wrap things up, in any shop . . .'

The tram reached the city. Angela woke with a great
start, rubbing at her eyes. She got out and stood
uncertainly on the traffic safety zone, looking dazedly
up at the town hall clock. Seymour handed back her
bag in silence, not mentioning the rose.

'Three o'clock!' she said. 'God, I never realised it was
that late! Listen, Seymour, I just remembered I've got
to see . . . I have an appointment and it's not one I
can break. I'm really sorry we're going to miss out on
lunch, you must be starving by now, but I'll take you
to McDonald's some other time. You'll be all right getting
back to Victoria Road by yourself, won't you? Just catch
the number fourteen tram and hop off at the stop past
that big pub on the corner. And you can't miss the
alley. That's practically opposite the tram stop where
you get out.'

The alleyway, he thought, harrowed. The dogs growling
behind the fences, that gang of kids – I can't . . . can't
walk down that place all by myself!

'What's the matter?' Angela asked. 'You've gone
peculiar looking. You feeling crook or something?'

Seymour nodded, snatching at the excuse with relief,
because there was no way he could explain about the
alleyway and his fear of walking along it alone.

'Oh hell! Look, I've got this appointment,' Angie said
impatiently. 'I've got to be there at three-fifteen on the
dot, and I've already broken the last one and they weren't
too rapt. I'll get shot if I don't show up today. Oh, come
on, Seymour, there's nothing to hopping on the number

51

fourteen tram and getting off at Victoria Road. It's not such a long trip, either, only about twenty minutes. You're not going to throw up right now, are you? Can't you last till you get home?'

'Couldn't I take a taxi instead of a tram?' Seymour said desperately. 'If you lend me the money, I'll pay you back. My mum's coming over on Friday and she'll give me some pocket money.'

Taxis would deliver you right to your front door, or at least not to Thelma's front door, for he couldn't even get in that formidable entrance with no key and the latticed barricade. But a taxi could take him up the alley, right up to the back gate, and the driver would be like a stalwart shield between him and all those terrors.

'Taxis? What do you reckon I am, a millionaire? God in heaven, as if I've got enough money for taxis! I already told you I was short of cash. It's only twenty minutes by tram, if that, you little pest!'

People milled about them on the traffic zone. Angie was tugged away from him in the tide, and he clung forlornly by one hand to the railing, thinking that she'd crossed with the stream of people and just left him adrift there like the useless piece of jetsam he was. But she surfaced again on his other side and took his free hand.

'Okay, then,' she said tersely. 'I'll come with you, only if you're going to throw up, don't do it all over Neptunia, right? You should have told me earlier you were feeling crook. Geeze, kids are pains! I think right now I've finally made up my mind never ever to be a mother!'

But she was nice to him on the fourteen tram, and when they reached Victoria Road, she didn't just dump him at the alley entrance and whisk off to her appointment. She walked all the way with him and he was ashamed of his deception which she so readily believed. An unseen dog barked and launched itself furiously against iron panels at the sound of their passing footsteps. He skittered around to the far side of Angela, hoping she didn't notice how his direction veered, or guessed the reason. Thelma had told him, sniping at modern manners, that men always used to walk on the gutter side of a street when out with women, so if a passing car splashed mud, the lady's dress wouldn't get dirty. Maybe Angie would think he was just being excessively polite, even if there was no traffic up the alley.

'You want to go in and take it easy,' she said when they reached Thelma's gate. 'Put a damp cloth on your forehead. Or eat some salt, isn't salt supposed to be good for heat exhaustion, or is that for something else? Anyhow, you run in and lie down.'

'Can I come over tomorrow?'

'Strewth, what do you think I'm running, a playgroup centre? Oh, all right, then . . . don't look like that, I didn't mean it. Tell you what, tomorrow I've got to go out and see my mother for her birthday, even if it is over. Want to come, too, if you're feeling up to it?'

'But . . . she won't want me there. She doesn't even know me.'

'Yeah, but I'd kind of like you along. She'll think you're a nice change from Jas and Rick and some of my other pals, that's for sure. It's sometimes . . . well, a bit difficult at my mum's. She gets a bit narked about things, can't say I blame her, but if I've got a mate along, a girlfriend or someone, she doesn't carry on quite so much. Nagging and that. I'll give her a ring and tell her there'll be one extra for lunch. You call in for me the same time as today, all right?'

She gave him a leg up over the gate and smiled, and he was charmed again by the grace of that smile. He sat for a moment on the top bar and watched her walk away up the alley, and knew she must have paid for that gold rose and there was no doubt about it. Someone as nice as Angela couldn't possibly be a thief.

Mum,

I love you, you know that. I'm so sorry, what I've done to the family, all the trouble I caused.

Listen, don't let Dad pay the fine, OK? I don't want to take any more money off him. I'll manage, a friend offered to help me out, it's OK, really.

It won't ever happen again, promise. Because I'm seeing this counsellor now, Judy put me on to him. I have a rave to him once a week in the city where he works and it's really helping. There's this self-help awareness group I heard about, too, might join it when I feel a bit better. (Not to worry, it's only some kind of gastro thing. Couldn't keep anything down, but it's clearing up now.)

Sorry about Rick and them phoning. I didn't give them our number, really and truly, they must have got it out of the phone book. Just hang up if they hassle you again, or tell them I've gone interstate.

I'll be OK, Mum, honest, don't worry so much, I feel fine, terrific!

Love ya, Angie.

P.S. I've got a great little flat now! Soon as I get it redecorated – it's pretty grotty looking at the moment – you and David and Lynne and Dad can come round for dinner. Only don't get your hopes up about the menu, you know what a flop I was in Home Eco at school!

## CHAPTER SIX

'I JUST WISH I STILL HAD MY little car!' Angie said as they walked up the long hill towards the hospital. 'You should have seen it, Seymour, it was a little VW painted mauve and I stuck daisy tranfers all over the bodywork. Only paid a couple of hundred, but it ran like a dream . . . oh, I miss that little bomb!'

'What happened to it?'

'Wrapped it around a power pole, total write-off. I went into a skid and next thing I knew there I was over this slope nearly into someone's front garden. Talk about freaky! There were all these live wires draped over the bonnet and no one could get me out. And faces . . . you know how a whole crowd always gathers when there's been an accident, can't miss out on a good old gawk, can they? Specially with an ambulance waiting just in case. Exhibit Number One, that was me! All these faces peering in at me and talking in low voices like I was going to panic or something. I wasn't panicky. It was sort of . . . well, like being in a dream. The only thing that worried me was maybe they wouldn't get me out safely. I'd had a bit of a domestic with Jas that morning and I thought that if I died, how sad it would be, the last thing he'd remember was me yelling and screeching and calling him every name under the sun. And then the cops turned up, naturally . . . I mean, they always do for an accident, but some of those guys remember number plates and . . . other stuff. They really have it in for you. Out for promotion, they never let up . . .'

Her face suddenly twisted with what seemed to Seymour to be irrational rage, but when she caught his eye she added quickly, 'Oh, these shoes are killing me! I shouldn't have worn them. I shouldn't have worn this top, either. Seymour, do you really think I look okay, you weren't just being smarmy?'

'You look all right, Angie, honest,' Seymour said. He thought she looked sensational in her gelati-striped shirt of lime green, bright yellow and pink. Her hair was caught up on top of her head with a twist of pink cord and spiked like a pineapple. He'd had an easy time choosing earrings to go with all that, for amongst the collection he'd actually found a pair of huge, yellow plastic pineapples.

'I'm not really sure about this top!' Angie said anxiously, still seeking reassurance. 'The neck's a bit . . . well, you know. I guess I should have worn Susan-Jane instead. My mum's always hassling me about the way I dress. She'd still like me to be wearing long white socks and tartan skirts.'

They reached the hospital and she told him again to wait outside by the goldfish pond. He watched the sad, introspective people seated on the veranda, then jumped, for Angie had returned and crept up behind him and was whispering evilly in his ear, 'Psst! Liddle boy, vant some nice candy?'

'Get lost, you old dero,' Seymour said. 'Who'd take candy from strange blokes wearing pineapple earrings?' Angie giggled, and he realised suddenly that he'd made a joke and caused someone to laugh, and he couldn't remember one other time in his life when that had happened.

She caught his hand and swung it as they went back down the main road. Seymour, unused to physical contact, felt woodenly self-conscious, but her hand held his lightly in uncomplicated friendship, and after a while he relaxed and swung in time to her singing. He wondered why kids at the various schools he'd attended so often spoke disparagingly about their sisters. If older sisters were as nice as Angie, making you feel special, as though they could think of nothing better than to spend their free time with you, he wished he'd been lucky enough to have one.

She sang all the way down the long road past the factories, and coaxed him into joining in. His voice, unaccustomed to being raised in melody, was no more than a feeble croak. He didn't know many songs at all, but she didn't laugh at him.

'Hey, heard this old one?' she said and began to sing, partly to him, mostly to herself, forgetting some of the words and having to improvise:

> 'I was weak, too weak to fly,
> But you were there, right there beside me,
> Urging me on . . .
>     Geeze, how does it go? And da da da . . .

Making me strong, could hear you saying . . .
    yeah, now I remember:
Spread my wings and left the nest,
Swearing nothin' would get by me.
I tasted love and I tasted life,
But not enough to satisfy me . . .
Urging me on, and making me strong,
Could hear you saying:
Go on, girl! You can do it, it's only life;
Ain't nothin' to it!
It's just a . . . a seeing-through it from the inside,
From the inside . . .'

Seymour listened, enchanted, for she had a sweet,
lilting voice, but when they came to the steep part
of the road leading to the bus terminal, she sang more
slowly, pausing for breath at the end of each line, so
that the tempo of the song changed and became almost
unbearably poignant and sad.

'Like a star in the midnight sky,
That fades into the morning;
Came back to show you I could fly,
But you had gone without a warning . . .
Could still hear you saying:
Go on, girl, you can do it,
It's only life . . .
It's just a seeing-through it from the inside,
From the inside . . .'

They reached the terminal and her voice dwindled
into silence. Seymour was relieved, because you didn't

sing in front of a crowd of people, though he had a suspicion that Angie might have no such scruples if she hadn't been made breathless by the long walk.

'Got to take a different bus this time, over to Merken,' she said. 'That's where my folks live. It's a bit boring, I should warn you, in case you're expecting something like Gresham Avenue. Oh, I used to hate Merken, you can't think how much!'

'What's wrong with it?'

'Merken's like . . . well, say one person gets ducted heating in their house, everyone else breaks their necks to do the same, not because they actually want ducted heating, but they can't bear to lag behind. That wouldn't do at all, the roof of the world might cave in. It's not really posh, but mind you, they're all working on it like grim death. Mortgageville, one of those subdivided places where they bunged up a whole lot of boring houses all alike so everything looks the same. I never really fitted in, you know. The only reason I go back is to see my family. Oh, I can hardly wait to have a good old natter with Lynne and David, I haven't seen them in months! Or Mum . . . Seymour, are you really sure I look okay?'

'Angie, you look just fine!' Seymour said, exasperated, but as the bus carried them through various suburbs towards Merken, she kept getting out her mirror and tweaking at her hair. She removed the pineapple earrings, then changed her mind and put them back in, and her fussing made Seymour, already uneasy at the thought of visiting strangers, even more jittery.

She'd bought a birthday card and opened it now to write a message inside. Her handwriting, Seymour thought, was like a little kid's, large and square and

60

painstaking, and the tip of her tongue was even protruding like a kid trying to get top marks in an exam as she wrote: 'To Mum, Happy Birthday, love from Angela, sorry I'm late with this card, but you know me – better late than never! Not like last year, heh?!! Lots of love and hugs and kisses.'

Merken was a gridwork of quiet streets lined with tidy, unexceptional houses, each set in a garden very much like the one next to it.

'I should have bought some flowers,' Angie said when they got off the bus. 'Mum always likes getting flowers for her birthday, Lynne never ever forgets. Oh, I should have remembered! It was crummy enough I forgot the proper date and she got worried when I didn't ring and Judy went and blabbed . . . but that's a long story. Well, I know how I can get round this one – hang on a jiff, Seymour!'

She stopped, looked around, then quickly broke several large stalks from a flowering shrub in someone's garden, assembling them with a rubber band from her handbag.

'What if whoever owned that garden came out and sprung you?' Seymour scolded. 'You shouldn't do things like that, Angie.'

'I know, you can't take me anywhere,' Angie said, walking on demurely. 'But I had an excuse all ready. I was going to say we were on the way to visit the cemetery and we didn't have any money to buy flowers for our granny's grave. You'd have to have a heart like a gargoyle to take flowers back off someone with a good excuse like that. Well, here's Acacia Avenue. All the streets round here are named after native flowers, original, huh?

This is our house and I bet that nosey old Mrs Duke next door is perving out through her Venetian blinds as usual. She'll be round to Mum's soon as we leave – "Oh, was that little Angela just called in? She hasn't been around for ages, has she, and isn't she putting on a lot of weight?" – Old cow. Seymour, you positive I look okay? Hey, you don't reckon I'm putting on weight, do you, not so you'd notice?'

'I only met you a couple of days ago.'

'Yeah, but . . .'

Seymour, however, had anxieties of his own. 'What do I call your mum?' he asked nervously, and wasn't reassured when Angie said, 'Well, her first name's Jeanette, but she's not the sort of person you can call by her first name straight off. So you'd better just settle for Mrs Easterbrook and be grateful.'

Mrs Easterbrook made Seymour feel welcome, but he sensed a texture in the atmosphere, as though Angela and her mother weren't quite comfortable with one another. Angie grew noticeably quieter and more decorous once inside the orderly house, as though attending some formal social event. Mrs Easterbrook seemed just as houseproud as Thelma, and even the cat bowl, he noticed, sat on a spotless white plastic mat instead of newspaper.

'I brought you a birthday present as well as these flowers,' Angie said. Mrs Easterbrook carefully undid the ribbon bow and smoothed and folded the gift wrapping before picking up the gold rose to look at it properly.

'Thank you, dear, it's lovely,' she said. 'It will look very nice in the china cabinet. I hope you didn't spend too much money, this looks as though it could have been very expensive.'

Seymour found himself staring at the floor, unable to meet anyone's eyes.

'Well, I wanted to get you something really fabulous and outdo David and Lynne,' Angie said. 'Why don't you put it up on the mantel? No one will be able to see it stuck away in the china cabinet. It would look great up on the mantel, Mum.'

'Dust would only collect in the petals,' Mrs Easterbrook said. She opened a corner cabinet and placed the rose carefully amongst a display of other pretty things and shut the door again. It was difficult to tell if she really liked her present or not. There were some beautiful ornaments in the cabinet, but they had the air of being locked away, not to be touched, and it seemed a pity that the rose, even if Angie – no, she must have paid for it – it seemed a pity that the elegant gold rose had to join them.

'I'll just make a salad dressing,' Mrs Easterbrook said. 'I'm afraid it's just quiche and salad, because you didn't give me much notice, Angie, otherwise I'd have planned something more elaborate. No thanks, dear, I don't need any help. Why don't you show Seymour where he can wash his hands before we eat?'

'Don't go thinking she means you've got germs,' Angie whispered as she took him up the hall. 'She thinks you might need the loo and you're too shy to ask, which would be just about spot on, anyhow. Hey, have a look in here, this used to be my old room when I was a kid.'

Seymour gazed through a doorway into a room so meticulously neat that it seemed to have no connection at all with the Angie he knew. The walls glowed with pale silken paper, white curtains floated like clouds at the windows where pastel blinds were drawn halfway down to exact levels. The room looked fresh and unused, as though nobody had ever lived in it at all.

'Mum's had it redecorated since I left home,' Angie said. 'You should have seen it when I had it, wow! Once I painted a big mural all over that wall. It was my tenth birthday and they said I could choose anything I wanted as a present, so that's what I asked for, to be allowed to paint a mural. And they couldn't back out, seeing they'd already promised. A tropical scene, that's what I did, palm trees and orchids and butterflies flitting about – geeze, I had a ball doing that!' She ran a hand wistfully over the pristine wallpaper. 'It's still there under this lot, you know, my mural. Bit sad, isn't it, all those poor butterflies locked away in the dark . . . Still, it's Mum's house, I guess she's allowed to do anything she wants with it.'

Mrs Easterbrook called them for lunch at a round table by a pair of French windows.

'Aren't we going to wait for . . .' Angie said and stopped, glancing down at the table. 'Oh, there's only three settings. What about Lynne and David? I'll get some more knives and forks out . . .'

'Lynne had a ballet class.'

'But she knew I was coming, didn't she? I haven't seen her for three months . . . Why didn't she stay home when she knew I was coming? She could have missed one lousy ballet class!'

'Angie . . .'

'And David, how come he's not here, either? Last

time I phoned he was in such a rush he didn't tell me anything, how he's getting on at school or anything at all. I wanted to see them both. I was really looking forward to today, everyone being here together and Seymour being able to meet them. Dave's going to show up, isn't he?'

'David had a dental appointment we couldn't very well cancel, it was arranged weeks ago. You know how hard it is to get an appointment in school holidays. Let's eat, shall we? Seymour, you sit over there, dear, and help yourself to the salad. Angie – oh, darling, do please put that cigarette out, you're getting ash all over the cloth – you haven't told me yet how you came to meet Seymour. Do you know his parents? I hope you've got permission to . . . Do you live near him?'

'Just over the way,' Angie said sulkily, not helping herself to salad when the bowl was passed. She looked annoyed and upset. 'Seymour gets a bit bored because he doesn't know any of the other kids in the street. Well, he sort of knows them, but they don't have a whole lot in common. He comes in to chat to me and we go out together now and then. I might take him to the beach tomorrow.'

'I can't swim,' Seymour blurted impulsively, but no one was listening.

'The beach?' Mrs Easterbrook said. 'I was under the impression that today was your rostered day off . . . Two free days in a row? Oh, I see, then I take it you're no longer working at that dress shop?'

'Oh, didn't I tell you about the shop?' Angie said, too casually. 'That old bitch who ran it . . .'

'Angela!'

'Oops, pardon me. That old dragon, there was a mix up about Bankcard slips and she went and blamed me and it was that really dumb junior there. Talk about teacher's pet and sucking up! Well, I opened my mouth and said a bit too much . . .'

'So you lost the job? How long ago?'

'Not all that long. It's no big deal, Mum. Okay, four weeks ago, but I'm not worried. I'll find something else pretty soon. Honest, I go through the employment ads every single morning without fail. Come on, let's talk about something else. Hey, want to hear about my new flat? A room, really, but flat sounds better. It's beaut, all self-contained and everything, isn't it, Seymour? He thinks it's terrific, always popping in for coffee. And it's got this little back gate into a sort of lane, so it's really private and peaceful. There's even a flower garden, well, a bush with flowers, anyway. Seymour picked some for me once . . . Jesus, Mum, why didn't Lynne and David show up for lunch? You did tell them I was coming, didn't you?'

There was a taut, fragile silence. Angie's face was suddenly pinched with distress, and Seymour found that he couldn't swallow one mouthful of quiche.

'Seymour, would you get a jug of water and some glasses from the kitchen, please? And some ice cubes, there's a tray in the freezer,' said Mrs Easterbrook. He went into the kitchen, knowing that he'd been sent out on purpose, but above the sound of the tap running he could still hear the conversation, lowered now into barbed whispers.

'You know what your father said. You're not to have any contact with them until you agree to go to Lakeview.'

'Oh, he's on about that again, is he? Look, I'm okay, I've told you a hundred times, told him a hundred thousand times. I'm on a program, and it's really working. It's been a whole two months since . . .'

'Just how many times have we heard that before, Angela?'

'Give us a break, will you?'

'Summonses turning up here for you, how do you think we felt . . .'

'They got their paperwork muddled up, honest, Mum. I'd already paid that fine, so I don't know what on earth they could have been carrying on about. It was only a piddling little parking offence. All right, then, *don't* believe me! I'm *not* going back to that Lakeview place. You don't know what it's like there, how they treat you, as though you just crawled out from under a compost heap. Jas reckons it's worse than being in . . .'

'Angela! I won't have that young man's . . .'

He'd filled and refilled the water jug several times over, had taken as long as anyone possibly could to detach ice cubes from a tray and find three glasses, and when he returned to the table, the brittle conversation stopped immediately. Angie smiled at him across the pretty lace cloth as he sat down – a bright smile, but her eyes above it were shining as though a film of tears lay close to the surface. Mrs Easterbrook had put the knife and fork down on the untouched food on her plate, and her face was filled with what seemed to be inexplicable, helpless pain. Seymour looked at all the beautifully prepared food on the table, poured himself a glass of water, then just sat, shoulders hunched, not knowing what to do.

I should start a conversation about the weather, he

thought miserably. About houses, maybe, interior decorating. Nice place you've got here, Mrs Easterbrook, that sort of stuff . . .

'Storm in a teacup,' Angie said lightly, and he could tell she was making an effort to salvage things. 'Every time I come here, it always ends in a squabble. Don't take any notice, Seymour. You know how families carry on. It's nothing. Mum, please don't let's argue, not when I brought Seymour out specially to meet you. He's a really great kid, a real gent. We're terrific mates, I'm going to take him to the zoo to see the butterfly house. Lots of places I'm going to take him . . .'

'Seymour,' Mrs Easterbrook said. 'If you've finished lunch, dear, you might like to play out in the back garden for a little while. Do you like cats? Ours should be around somewhere out there.'

Seymour recognised an order, a dismissal. He left the table meekly and went out through the kitchen door and into the garden. It was an attractive one and someone had lavished much care and attention upon it, but it somehow didn't look the sort of place you'd play in. And the cat turned out to be an aloof black sphinx who desired no company. He could tell by the disdainful way it dampened a paw and began to groom its face that he was meant to keep his distance. Besides, how could you play with a cat? he thought crossly. No one could tell cats what to do or how to behave. The sun-warmed rim of the patio was too hot for comfort, so he moved back into the wall shadow next to the windows, and knew at once he'd made an error. He could quite clearly hear Mrs Easterbrook and Angie talking; not talking, but having a passionate, bitter quarrel

68

now that he'd been sent from the room. He stayed where he was against the wall, afraid that if he moved they'd hear and think he'd come to that place on purpose to eavesdrop. He tried not to listen, but the angry voices crackled against the windows like flames.

'What can you expect after what you've put us through for the last five years? All the times you've promised . . . We've given you every chance in the world, Angela, all our help, and you just threw away every opportunity . . .'

'For God's sake, how many times are you going to bring that up?'

'Look at you, dressed like a little tramp! Those clothes, you can't even make the effort to look respectable when you come to visit. How do you think I feel, with Margaret Duke seeing you stroll in here dressed like that? Those abominable shoes, and your hair . . . Why on earth don't you let it grow back to its natural colour? Oh, you had such beautiful hair! That job your father got you, the one before this dress shop fiasco, you made absolutely no effort . . .'

'A fortnight was plenty long enough, thanks very much! Dad wouldn't even listen when I tried to explain what happened. That horrible old woman told all her friends about me, I heard her. Making out she was so Christian, it just about made me puke! Every time she went out, even just up to the shops, she'd lock away all her brooches and stuff, how do you reckon that made *me* feel? Some job, a home help! I only took it on to please Dad in the first place, and I tried, I really tried. It wasn't my fault . . .'

'It never is your fault, is it? We've just about reached the end of our tether with you, Angela. Well, no doubt we're being fools and wasting money, but as I've explained, we're willing to pay your fares up to Lakeview again. Only this time you've got to promise to stay there for at least . . .'

'Mum, give it a break, will you? Please?'

'Oh, Angela . . . oh, my darling . . . It doesn't have to be like this! If you'd only stayed there the first time, given it a proper chance . . . Can't you just . . .'

'Look, damn it, it didn't work out! I can't stand being shut up like that. You don't even know what it's like there. You only hear that smug counsellor all sweetness and light over the phone – as if she'd know anything about it! I'm getting it all together and staying out of strife, what more can you ask? Six weeks I've lasted this time plus I've found somewhere nice to live, why can't you at least give me credit for that?'

'Do you call a court appearance getting it all together? How do you think we felt when that lawyer rang the last time?'

'They plant stuff in your handbag. I never . . .'

'Angela, I've heard the same pathetic lie so many times I'm not prepared to listen to it any more! You're just lucky you managed to get off with a good-behaviour bond, and next time you needn't expect your father to pay for a top lawyer. You can just take your chances with Legal Aid. Oh, what's the use, you never give a thought to all the trauma you've caused us! All our love, and you just keep throwing it back in our faces. We've got rights, too, you know, as parents, as a family . . .'

'Okay,' Angie said coldly. 'I get the message loud and clear. I guess I'd better shove off before Lynne and David come home, isn't that what you want? You wouldn't want me around contaminating them, would you? I bet they didn't even have any ballet lessons or dental appointments at all, it was you and Dad making sure they were kept out of my way! I came out here to tell you something, but I guess it's not the right time. Maybe it won't ever be the right time. Maybe it won't even happen, anyhow. I think I'd better just take myself off now, okay?'

'The only good news you could tell me is that you've booked yourself into Lakeview and you're prepared to stay there for as long as it's necessary,' Mrs Easterbrook said heavily over the scrape of a chair being thrust back from the table.

Seymour crept off the patio and out into the middle of the lawn and pretended to be looking at a rockery, so that when Angie called him, she wouldn't guess he'd overheard that anguished conversation which wasn't meant for anyone else's ears. At the front door as they went out, Mrs Easterbrook's face was composed and neutral, and she even chided Angie gently for wearing such tight jeans instead of a cool dress in the heat, but not in a nagging way. Angie bent forward to kiss her on the cheek, but Mrs Easterbrook just held her face still, suffering the kiss, not returning it, and the door closed before they even reached the front gate.

Mrs D. Rusden
Supervisor
Mountain Gate Child Minding Centre
Mountain Highway
Elthwick

Dear Mrs Rusden,
   I'd like to apply to for the position of Child-
care Worker you advertised last week. I haven't
had any experience professionally in this area,
but I know I could handle it very well. I really
like kids and being with them, and I have a
younger brother and sister I used to babysit for.
   Previous jobs include the following: Working
at a race stable; ~~flower stall assistant~~ florist;
dress shop assistant; ~~barmaid~~ waitress; pizza hut
~~assistant~~ manageress; vet's receptionist; home
help for an elderly lady. (Unfortunately, as I've
moved recently, I can't enclose copies of
references as the box they were in is still in
storage). However, I would appreciate it very
much if I was given the chance of an interview. I
can begin work at any time and also work
flexible hours if you like. I'm sorry I don't have
the phone on yet for you to contact me, but
either of the two people mentioned below will
pass on any messages.

Yours sincerely,

Angela Fleur Easterbrook.

1) *Judy Anderson, Tel. 656 1123*
2) *Rick Harkmann, Tel. 798 7756*
*P.S. I'd really love working in a creche and am very anxious to find a steady job. I know it wouldn't matter that I've had no experience working in a creche before, as I'm a hard worker and learn things really fast!*

Big White Mansion
Gresham Avenue
Nobbs Hill
Sunday or something

Hey, Seymour, little buddy!
Don't even know if you were planning to pop around, but let yourself in with the spare key if I haven't got back yet. Had to go out unexpectedly. Don't take any notice of the pair of jeans soaking up the water in the fridge (defrosting it and couldn't find the drip tray thing)!
I left a Mars bar and some marshmallows on the sink for you – (Vant some nice candy, liddle boy?)
Hey, heard this joke?
Q: What's the difference between 'Ugh!' and 'Ugh! Ugh!'
A: 'Ugh!'
(Pretty sick, huh?)
See ya, don't go away if I'm not there. Be back as soon as I can and I'll bring us both a yummy pizza and all the trimmings for afternoon tea!

Love from Angie

P.S. Have you got rid of that DAGGY shirt yet?!!! Don't go putting it in the charity bin, either, you'll have all the derros chasing you round town trying to hit you over the head with wine bottles.

P.P.S. Hey, we could go up the market one day and buy you some fantastic tee shirts, saw one there with the Phantom on it and his eyes light up behind this mask.
P.P.P.S. Hope this letter doesn't land on Thelma's head by mistake if she's hanging up the washing! Couldn't find a stone to weigh it down with, so I want this elephant earring back!

## CHAPTER SEVEN

HIS MOTHER CAME FOR HER promised visit and stayed the weekend. There were many secretive, murmured conferences between her and Thelma in the front room, with Seymour banished to the kitchen to make endless pots of tea. In between the conferences in which he had no part, his mother kept insisting how wonderful it would be when they were back together at the end of the month, how the new situation at Carrucan would make up for these four trying, solitary weeks. Seymour made agreeable responses, but kept his mind perfectly blank, not allowing any expectations to take seed. He knew just how stark the gap between imagination and reality could be.

She took him out on Saturday, but it wasn't an enjoyable excursion. Even the start of it was charged with drama. First she opened the front door a crack and peered through, then went dramatically to the gate to check that his father wasn't lurking about in Victoria Road. And when they travelled into the city, most of the time was spent in buying new school clothes. The only emotion Seymour felt when he tried on the new uniform was a detached curiosity about how much wear he'd actually get out of it before they moved on to some other place.

Uniforms, he thought dully, were really only suitable for kids who lived predictable ordinary lives. In nice predictable ordinary suburbs where nothing ever altered except someone building a new garage, someone else having an extra room added to their house. That's what his mother wanted, to live in a place like that. She'd keep such a house so trim, too, as neat as a little cuckoo clock. Suddenly he noticed how she glanced at certain things on display in the store – curtain material, cushions – and in those glances he thought he detected the same degree of yearning he'd experienced himself over objects. It was . . . sad.

He raged silently at his father, seeing him as a useless wastrel, a no-hoper. It wasn't too much to ask, a permanent home somewhere, a job like everyone else's father. Only . . . a memory edged into his mind, of the little fold-down table in the caravan and a newspaper spread out at the employment ads, some of them ringed with pencil. Seymour, almost asleep in the top bunk, had watched the pencil suddenly roll away from tired fingers and drop to the floor. He had watched his father's hands go up to his temples, and the worry lines across his forehead deepen into something like despair.

There was no way they'd ever all live together in a little cuckoo-clock house in a garden suburb like – well, Merken, where Angie had grown up. Only, perhaps it didn't matter all that much, anyhow. There hadn't been much evidence of happiness in Angie's former house.

She hadn't liked it, she'd moved on. Perhaps it was as he'd suspected all along, no place was ever going to be any good, and you just had to come to terms with it.

Maybe he'd been wrong about his mother hankering after curtain fabric and cushions. She certainly wasn't now – she was hurrying him briskly towards the cafeteria, pleased with herself because she'd found some needle-work stuff at half-price on a display counter. All those little mats she made, he thought, sitting down to lunch. Why does she bother? She's got no house full of tables and shelves to put mats on, no place of her own . . . But she chatted, with what seemed like enthusiasm, of the new job and the possibility of it being permanent if things worked out as she thought they might.

'We could even get some of our stuff out of storage,' she said. 'Take it along with us when we move, just in case. There's my little chintz chair . . . Don't put your elbows on the table, Seymour, you know better than that.'

'What if . . .' Seymour began, intending to say, 'What if Dad gets that maintenance job at the golf links he was talking about, aren't you going to give him another chance? Aren't we all all going to be living back together again?'

'Don't talk with your mouth full,' said his mother. 'Goodness, I hope you haven't been doing that at Thelma's. She'll think I haven't brought you up properly. I don't want you getting into sloppy habits, dear. It was a mistake letting you go to your father even for that short time. I don't know, every time I go against my better judgment and let you visit – not that he deserves it – what was it you wanted to say?'

'Nothing.'

After lunch in the department-store cafeteria, they went to a film, but not one of his choosing, for his mother had already booked the tickets. Going to the movie was his birthday outing treat, and the school clothes, a five-dollar note and new pencil box were his gifts.

The rest of the weekend seemed interminable, just more whispered conversations which changed to facile general chat when he brought in fresh pots of tea. He gathered that some sort of legal custody action was being planned, but his mother didn't tell him any details. He was even relieved when Monday morning came and she left at the same time as Thelma.

No one answered his knocking when he went across to visit Angie at ten-thirty, although the door wasn't locked. He put his head inside to investigate and saw that she was still half asleep.

'Angie . . . hey, Ange, wake up! You'll be late picking up your medicine at the hospital,' he said, but she only muttered something about it being too late, that he should nick off and for God's sake leave her alone, and slumbered on. The room was even more untidy than usual. Quietly, being careful not to disturb her, he filled in time by straightening up the kitchen section. He tackled the washing up and scrubbed a patina of grime from the little sink. Then he glanced uncertainly at Angie, who had slept through all the subdued clatter of things being made orderly. She looked ill, her eyes circled by dark rims like bruising, and apparently she hadn't bothered to change into a nightgown, but had just tumbled fully clad into bed the previous night. He made coffee and took it to the bedside.

'Come on, now, lazy,' he coaxed. 'You can't stay in bed sleeping all day. How about what you told your mum, that you were going to look for a job?'

It took many persistent shakes, but finally Angie opened her eyes and sat up and glared at him. Groaning quietly, she sipped the coffee and lit a cigarette. The ashtray by the bed was choked with stubbed cigarettes and ash, so he emptied it into the kitchen rubbish bin and brought it back clean. Angie didn't thank him or even seem to notice.

'You could still make it out to the hospital if you get a move on,' he said, for punctuality and routine had been instilled in him all his life by his mother and it made him edgy when people deviated from it. 'You said you had to pick up that medicine every day, Angie.' He paused and added, without looking at her, 'What sort of stuff is it? What's it for?'

'Told you that already, and don't nag, my head can't stand it . . .' Angie snapped. 'My metabolism. I'm giving the hospital a miss this morning. No point. I don't think I've quite got the hang of today, yet. Thanks for the coffee, anyway.' Her hands shook, splashing coffee and ash on to the blanket, and Seymour dabbed ineffectually with a tissue from the bedside table.

'Sit down,' Angie said irritably. 'Don't be darting about like Sadie the cleaning lady. You'll end up a fuddy-duddy old bachelor before you even reach your teens if you don't watch out.'

The chair was piled with clothes, so he perched awkwardly on the end of the bed, feeling depressed because the day wasn't turning out as he'd planned. He'd been looking forward to choosing earrings to match

80

whatever she planned to wear, hadn't even minded about the lengthy trip to the hospital, for after that was over they could have gone somewhere else and spent a cheerful, bright afternoon.

Angie certainly didn't look cheerful now, and he thought of the quarrel she'd had with her mother, all those things he'd overheard and didn't understand, or only half understood. They fluttered softly about in his mind like bats in a cave, but suddenly alarmed, not wanting to know, he pushed those thoughts into a separate compartment and slammed the shutters down. Angie smiled at him over the coffee, a wan shadow of her usual joyful smile, but his spirits lifted a little.

'So, where'd you get to yesterday, Buster?' she said moodily. 'Standing me up, eh? I could have taken you to the zoo, you know. There's this cute orang-outang there. He's got this old chaff-bag like a security blanket and he just sits with it over his head, like he's got it lined with rude postcards or he can't bear the sight of the world. He kills me, that orang-outang. Only you didn't show up . . .'

'But I told you I couldn't drop in over the weekend, Angie, don't you remember? It was when we were coming back from your mum's, that's when I told you. I had to go into town for school things.'

'Oh, well, maybe you did tell me, my mind's like a colander. I had a sort of busy weekend myself, anyway. Ran into some mates I hadn't seen for ages. We went . . . went . . .' Angie wrinkled her forehead, shook her head as though it were too much of an effort to remember and slid down with her arms folded behind her tousled head. She stared through the tiny window at the patch

81

of cornflower sky, and seemed to forget that he was there. Her face emptied of everything else except melancholy.

'You look sort of white, Angie, like you've got the flu or something,' Seymour said. 'Maybe it's not a bad idea if you got your act together and went out to that hospital and saw a doctor.'

'Doctors,' she scoffed. 'The ones at that hospital aren't any good. They're jerks out there. I reckon they've all been deregistered for funny business, and they've snuck in again through the back door. It's the pits, that clinic, stuck all the way out on North Road. They expect people to hold down jobs and still get out there every day somehow, and they don't dare be ten minutes late. Doctors only tell you things you don't want to know about. I'll be okay, you don't have to worry about me. I might get up later and do a few things, but right now I'll just lie here and rest. I feel really tired . . . Oh God, I feel so damned tired . . .'

'Do you want me to go, then?' Seymour asked, thinking of Thelma's house and the hours of arid boredom that waited for him across the alley.

'No, you don't have to scarper. Stay and talk to me, keep me company. Keep me comforty, that's what my little sister used to say when she was learning to talk. Cute, eh? When she was sick in bed she'd say, "Don't go to school, Angie, stay home and keep me comforty." Lynne's pretty, isn't she? Talented, too. She'll get a place in any ballet company she applies to when she's older, no doubts about that. She's got one of those ballet faces, you know the sort of faces those girls always have, neat and pure like flowers. Didn't you reckon she was pretty?'

'But Angie, I never met . . .'

'It's beaut having a little sister, though I guess fourteen isn't little any more. And my brother David, he's a real whizz with maths and computers and stuff like that. You should have seen the things he used to make when he was only in primary school. Good at sport, too. Takes after my dad, he's pretty smart as well. High achievers, that's what my family's all about – did you just happen to notice all those trophies and certificates and stuff on the mantel, cups for this and that?'

'Yes, I saw them.'

'I'm the odd one out. Not that they ever let me feel it, mind. I mean, they weren't always staring at me over the table and saying things like, "What a shame Angie's so dumb, maybe there could have been a mix-up at the maternity hospital when she was born." Nothing like that, I haven't got that as an excuse . . . oh hell, all it takes is one lousy party! Just one lousy rotten party and showing off, wanting to sparkle like a Christmas tree . . . Little smartypants Angie, in over her neck . . . I must have been a very big disappointment to my family, you know. I didn't win anything, even when I was in Brownies. Only ever got one badge for First Aid and that's just because the lady doing the testing was a friend of mum's, so she couldn't very well not pass me.'

'I never won anything, either,' Seymour said. 'At school or anywhere else. I guess it's because we move round a lot. It's rotten. I don't mean not winning stuff, but you don't stay anywhere long enough to make friends, either. Not that I'm much good at that. Kids sort of pick on you when you're new.'

'Only if you let them. You're not tough enough, Seymour.'

'Can't help it. I don't know how to . . . you know, stand up to people.'

'Well, you don't have to be a prize fighter all covered in battle scars. There's other ways of coming out top – you've just got to outsmart people when they start to hassle you, be one jump ahead. Sort of talk your way out of things if you can't do it the other way. Like having a secret weapon.'

Seymour contemplated that advice dubiously and didn't think it applied to him. He saw himself as a soldier with no weapons at all, secret or otherwise. Someone had forgotten right from the start to equip him with any weapons and soon there would be another stage in that long haphazard march.

'Got my new school uniform yesterday,' he said glumly. 'Geeze, I'm dreading it. You just get used to one teacher and then you have to move on to some place else and start all over again . . .'

'Some place else and start all over again . . .' Angie murmured, and sighed.

Seymour remembered his pencil case and took it out of the paper bag to show her. A birthday gift, even if this wasn't a spectacular one, was after all something out of the ordinary. The pencil case was made of stone-grey fabric with a strong zip, utilitarian, practical as concrete. As he gazed at it, he wished suddenly he hadn't brought it across the alley, after all. 'Got this for my birthday on Saturday,' he explained, embarrassed.

'It's . . . very nice,' Angie said politely, then she grinned, then burst out laughing. 'Seymour, who gave

84

it to you, the Gospel Hall Benevolent Fund? It's exactly like something those nerdy kids at school would have, you know those kids – every school has them, always sucking up to teachers and putting the date on their work without being told and they never let you have a loan of their coloured pencils.'

'And they're picked to ring the bell and take messages round the classrooms,' Seymour said.

'Their socks always stay up. I reckon they use glue.'

'And they never let you cheat off their work in tests.'

'In fact they always sit with their elbows over their work even if you weren't planning to cheat!' Angie finished.

Seymour put the pencil case away, not minding about it so much any more, because it had become funny in some special way and he felt cheered. 'I always do get given stuff like this,' he said ruefully. 'At Christmas it was socks and a new dressing-gown. A Victoria Road Gospel Hall Benevolent Fund sort of dressing-gown.'

'You should have told me it was your birthday on the weekend. I'd have bought you something really terrific, certainly not socks or pencil cases. A skull bed lamp, maybe . . . Or a dragon kite, or a trip up in a hot-air balloon. I feel rotten not knowing it was your birthday. I must have something I can give you, let's think . . .'

'It doesn't matter, Angie. You don't have to.'

'Yes, I do. It's low-down and mean to miss out on a friend's birthday. I know . . . it's not much, and it's fallen down behind the bedside table so it might be a bit squashed, but . . . I knew it was here somewhere! Happy birthday, Seymour.'

It was a small picture in a cardboard frame with splodges of Blu-Tak on the edges. Seymour held it in his hands and looked at it. It was three-dimensional, made of layers of clear liquid-filled plastic in which glittering specks floated. Behind the specks was a little white horse with outspread wings, poised above a silvered, turreted landscape pin-pricked with stars. The effect was mysterious and beautiful, like a landscape on a different planet. When he moved the card gently, the little horse seemed to raise its wings and fly, and all the time, miniscule silver rain fell around it.

'Hey, thanks, Angie!' he said. 'It's fantastic! I've never seen anything like this before. Except . . .'

'Except what?'

'It's a bit like that tattoo you've got on your shoulder.'

'Oh, that,' Angie said. 'Yes, well I'm sort of sorry I had that done. It's too noticeable – people remember you when you don't particularly want them to. Pegasus, that's the name of that little flying horse. Wouldn't it be terrific to have a real one? Just hop on its back when things get rough and take off up into the sky where no one can ever . . . I used to have that picture pinned up in my room when I was a kid at home. Time I got shot of it, I'm a big girl now, though that's a debatable point. I'm glad you like it and it's found a new owner. Listen, you haven't chosen which earrings I should wear today yet. I had to wear these pineapple ones all weekend because you didn't show up to pick me out a new pair. Didn't get round to it myself. How'd you like to have big chunky pineapples stuck in your ears when you're sick and have to stay in bed?'

Seymour fetched the jewellery box and chose small

red plastic bells. She put them on and inspected herself in a hand mirror.

'Somehow they just don't go with my face this morning,' she said. 'Oh, heck, I look like something that just tottered out of a geriatric ward! All I need is dentures and a walking frame. I should get up and have a shower, only if I moved I think maybe my head might fly off. That's what it feels like, no kidding.'

'Maybe you'd feel a bit better if you had some breakfast.'

'You and your nagging. That's all I need at this hour.' She made a wobbly effort to rise, but sank back to the edge of the bed, arms wrapped about herself, shivering. 'It's no use,' she said flatly. 'I feel too sick to have a shower, even. I'd better just hop back into bed. Sorry, mate, not being able to take you out somewhere for a birthday treat. Sorry, love . . . Tomorrow, maybe.'

'That's okay. But you'd better have something to eat, Angie. How about I cook something up for you.'

'I don't know what I've got in the fridge. Can't remember if I shopped on Saturday or not, that's when I usually go down to the market. I just can't remember Saturday, it's like it never happened. Maybe it didn't.'

There was nothing in the fridge except a carton of milk and some oranges. He searched through the cupboards but found nothing much there, either, and when he turned around Angie had dozed off again on the pillow. Her face wasn't the calm face of a person asleep, it was troubled and unhappy, fighting bad dreams. Seymour went back across the alley to Thelma's house. He took a can of tomato soup and some slices of bread from the kitchen, hoping their absence wouldn't be noticed, and returned to Angie's place. The soup turned lumpy because the only saucepan he could find to cook it in had an uneven base, but he toasted the bread under the griller and arranged everything neatly on the tray. Angie woke up – or perhaps she hadn't really been asleep at all behind that restless face – and tried to eat the lunch he'd prepared, but left most of it on the tray.

'You're still shivering,' Seymour said. 'Thelma's got a hot-water bottle in her laundry. Want me to go over and get it?'

'Geeze, you're sweet,' Angie said huskily, gazing at him over the lunch she hadn't eaten. 'No, I don't want a hot-water bottle, but thanks anyhow, pal. You're looking after me as though I'm your own mum or something like that . . .'

'My mother never stays in bed when she gets sick,' Seymour said and thought of her, sharp and slim as a needle, darting through his life. 'She just takes an Aspro and keeps going. She reckons everything would fall apart in our family if it wasn't for her,' he added, unsure if it were something to be proud of or otherwise, and thinking it had all fallen apart, anyway, in spite of her taut, brittle energy.

'Well, I guess she wouldn't approve of me, then, slouching around like this. I'll have to pull my socks up a bit when I have . . . Jas and me are going to get married just as soon as things work out, and you never know, I just might have a kid straight off. Sooner than I planned, even, with my rotten luck. What do you think about that, me being a mum? Freaky, isn't it, the whole idea? Still, you can be its uncle if you like. I mean if it even happens.'

Seymour didn't know anything much about babies, but once he'd been in a queue at the post office behind a young mother. The baby she'd held had made him uncomfortable by staring at him fixedly with clear blue eyes, like glass buttons. But then, with no invitation on his part, it had suddenly smiled right into his face, an unpractised smile like someone learning to drive, but one of incredible sweetness and trust. Not knowing him, not knowing anything about him, even his name, but it had focused its clear eyes on his face and smiled like that. He still remembered how pleased and almost honoured he'd felt.

'Of course, I'll have a proper house by then,' Angie said. 'Something will turn up. Couldn't possibly have a baby in this place, could I? That house we saw in Gresham Avenue, that'll be the one. That'll do to keep the rain out. My baby's only going to have the best, right from the start.'

'What would you call it?'

'Names? Heavens, I haven't got as far as that yet. I haven't even decided whether to . . . Why, what do you think I should call it – that is, if I ever do decide to have a kid?'

Seymour tried to remember names from all the schools he'd attended. There had been a kid, way back when he was in Year Three and starting halfway through a term when everyone already knew everyone else. He still remembered that girl's name, Melissa Miller, and the way she'd given him a bunch of grapes from her lunch box.

'How about Melissa?'

'Yes, that's nice. What if it's a boy, though? Tell you

what, we could start making a list, and put down any good name we come up with. You never know, that list might come in handy sooner than expected. Melissa. We'll definitely grab that one because you thought of it.'

She printed Melissa on a new page in a polka-dot covered memo book from her handbag. They both became so involved with listing names that a whole half hour passed, and Angie regained some of her sparkle. She began making up improbable, far-fetched names.

'Cinnamon,' she said. 'Or how about Lancelot – that'd suit him if he turns out to be a famous surgeon.'

'That's sick. Archibald would do for when he's a baby,' Seymour said. 'Babies don't have much hair.'

'Get out, my baby's going to have the most beautiful hair in the world, right from the start. How about Tressaline? Or something really different – Pegasus. Bet no one's ever been called that. Pegasus Tressaline Lancelot . . .'

'Miss Reynolds,' someone called, and rapped sharply on the door. 'Miss Reynolds, I'd like a word with you, please.'

Angie tensed, her pink tasselled pencil scribbling to a halt. 'Oh, shivers, it's the old dragon about the rent!' she whispered in consternation.

'But your name's not . . .'

'Never mind about that now! Listen, be a sport and tell her I'm asleep, got an appendicitis attack, anything . . . just get rid of her for me, there's a honey.' She shot down under the blankets, placed one hand over her eyes and gave an incredibly good performance of someone locked into a sleep so critical that permanent illness might result from its interruption.

Seymour had no time to retreat into his usual fazed shyness. He found himself opening the door to a pugnacious woman who glowered at him suspiciously.

'She's not feeling well,' Seymour stammered, eyes cast down. The woman's shoes were enormous and looked as though they could easily force a way into the room past his frail defences, with the same ruthless authority as battle ships. 'She's got . . . a very bad attack of flu. The doctor said she had to have plenty of sleep. I'm looking after her.'

'Oh, and who are you?'

'I'm . . . her brother. Just visiting, it's school holidays . . .'

'Would you mind telling her, please, that her rent's overdue?' said the cross lady. 'I made it quite clear it was to be paid on the first Thursday of each month. That was our arrangement, and this is the second time she's been late.'

'Okay, I'll tell her, but I'm sorry, she's fast asleep right now. The doctor gave her . . . what do you call them, antibiotics. He said I was to let her sleep and not wake her up. It's the only way to deal with flu, you can get serious complications.' The little snippets of information gleaned from listening to years of his mother's medical talk rolled off his tongue like oil.

The woman on the doorstep shot him an annoyed, frustrated look, but just said, 'Very well. I'll leave it for now, but when she wakes up, you make sure she knows to drop that rent in by tomorrow morning at the latest. Plenty of other people are after a nice flat like this one.'

Seymour nodded and shut the door, then went back to the bed. 'Angie, why didn't you help me out?' he said indignantly. 'That was a rotten thing to do, letting me cop all that! It's dumb, forgetting to pay your rent, you get a bad name. My mum never . . . I reckon you'd better get up and go in and pay her right now!'

But Angie, he discovered, was truly asleep, not shamming at all. The hand had fallen from her eyes and lay tangled in her damp, tumbled hair. She was drifting somewhere a long way from him, almost as though she'd floated away to that silvered landscape in his picture, had drifted away to the huge spinning rings of Saturn. All his exasperated, worried mutterings couldn't bring her back, so after a while he pulled the blind down so the sun wouldn't burn her face, shut the door behind him and went back dejectedly across the alleyway to Thelma's house.

REDECORATING IDEAS:
pink wallpaper with rose pattern
mirror tiles in shower recess (fix hole in wall first)
fluffy pink mat and matching towels from market
turn bed into settee with rose cover and
    matching cushions
row of potplants painted white on windowsill
get decent cutlery and kitchen stuff
new curtains – or stripey pink/white blind?
paint wardrobe with gloss enamel, gold knobs
waste paper basket covered with stickers
cane rocking chair from secondhand shop painted
    gloss white
patchwork cushion
COST?!!
Won't be here all that long, anyway, waste of money!!!
TO HELL WITH IT!!!!

Angie,

Honestly, I'm sorry I was such a bitch on the phone, and maybe I shouldn't have hung up on you, but – you've got a NERVE even asking. That bracelet was Grandma's. Mum would notice straight away if I wasn't wearing it or if it wasn't around. No, I won't let you borrow it! Take that as final! Plus all that bulldust about wanting to wear it somewhere special doesn't fool me for one little moment, either. It would be the little pearl studs all over again, wouldn't it?

Come on Angie, just when are you going to get yourself out of this rotten mess? Sometimes I get so MAD at you! When's it all going to stop? Quit asking me to do things behind their backs, OK? I know all the stuff Gran left is pretty yuk, but she meant it to be passed on to you and me and then our kids, kept in the family. I won't let you take any of it away.

Ange, if you don't want to give Lakeview another try, there was this other place I read about in the paper. Run by some church, can't remember what religion, but they're all into meditation and health food and that. The cure rate they've got there is really high, 60% or something like that. I cut out the article and I'll send it to you with this letter care of Judy, seeing I don't know your new address. I don't know why I bother, though. I get so MAD at you.

Mum was so upset when you came out and said all those awful things, she cried for hours after you'd gone. I found her crying over all your

baby photos, for heaven's sake! That was
horrible, turning up here dressed like that,
making a scene, what are you trying to prove,
Angie?

No, I won't 'lend' you that little gold bracelet,
don't go ringing me up again when you know
they're all out, either, you'll just get the phone
slammed down in your ear again.

Angie, I get so sad, give them a break, all
right? Dad's starting to look so old and tired.
Give us all a break, damn you!

Lynne

Dear Jas,

You know I want to keep it, you know how I feel about kids. Maybe it would work out, hey? I could go on the supporting parents benefit or whatever it's called like Judy did. She's managing OK and she got a Min. of Housing flat, too, you should see how she's done it up.

Jas, write and tell me what I should do.

You owe me about a hundred letters already, you lazy slob (Anyone would think your time isn't your own! Joke.) Oh Jas, I miss you!

North Road's not too bad, apart from that bitch Marilyn who's in charge, she really looks down her nose when you front up every day. Rick was keeping me company out there, but he got kicked off the program (surprise surprise). I'm going really well, you'd be so proud of me!

Judy said to say hello (only not all that enthusiastically). She keeps pretty much to herself these days. You should see her baby, Amy Siobhann she called it, it's so sweet! Amy was OK at birth, didn't even have to go into intensive care and the birth weight was fine, how lucky can you get, eh? Jude's going great guns, she's even given up smoking as well! Maybe it would work out for me, too.

Haven't told my folks yet, don't know how to. How can I tell them, I don't even know what I'm going to do yet!!! Have to make up my mind pretty soon, hey?

Jas, please write and tell me what I should do.
Love ya always,

Angie

'I NEVER LET THAT OLD witch worry me,' Angie said airily. 'If you're even five minutes late with the rent, she flaps about wringing her hands like someone out of an opera. I already fixed it, so don't remind me about it on a beautiful day like this. I thought we came out to have some fun. That's why I wore Carmen Miranda.' Carmen Miranda was a short, tiered skirt of different colours, resembling three bright parasols placed one on top of another, and a red shirt tied in a knot at the waistline. 'Though you wouldn't know who Carmen Miranda was unless you watch old midday movies,' Angie added. 'She used to wear her hair all piled up with tropical fruit ornaments and danced the rumba. And her earrings – they were fabulous! Today I'm going to shout myself a new pair of earrings.'

'Can you afford it?' Seymour asked automatically, because his mother was fond of saying, 'Need, not Greed. First work out if you really need something, and you'll find out that ninety-nine per cent of the time you can get by without it.'

But Angie seemed merrily oblivious of sayings like 'Need, not Greed'. After they'd called in at the North Road hospital and returned to the bus terminal, she went into a nearby shop and looked at cheap jewellery. Seymour found himself covertly watching, feeling diminished a little by his action, to make sure that she really did pay for the items she finally chose. She certainly seemed to have plenty of money in the little silver mesh purse she drew out of her handbag. It bulged with the weight of notes and coins. She bought a pair of earrings shaped like gaudy parrots and put them on in the shop. As well as the earrings, she bought two little china ballet slippers attached to each other with pink ribbon. Seymour privately thought they were pretty useless, but Angie seemed to adore them and asked for them to be gift wrapped with a shiny rosette to seal the parcel.

'Now,' she said, pulling him on to a bus just as it was about to move off. 'Out we go to East Merken. We're meeting someone there and I'm shouting you both to lunch. You can order anything you like and second helpings, too.'

Seymour immediately shrank away from the thought of meeting another person, a stranger, and having to make conversation. Angie wouldn't tell him who it was and laughed at his reluctant face.

'You look just like Morris Carpenter,' she teased.

'Who's he?'

'This freaky kid when I was in primary school. Heavens, I'd nearly forgotten all about old Morris Carpenter! You should have seen him, he was the most miserable gloomy kid in the whole world. I reckon when he was born the first thing he would have done was throw a punch at the nurse. Middle of summer, on days just like this one, there he'd be all bundled up in a duffel coat, no kidding. And if you ever felt sorry for him and asked him to join in things, he'd just sort of glare at you and then he'd croak, "Why should I?" '

Angie gave such a good imitation of a surly voice growling, 'Why should I?' that the passenger in the seat in front turned around to stare, but Angie didn't seem troubled at attracting attention. She went on scowling at Seymour, the contours of her face yanked down into gloom and doom. Still being Morris Carpenter, she rattled the thin silver bangles on her wrist contemptuously. 'Look at this rubbish,' she sneered. 'A person can probably get lumpy old eczema from wearing metal. Not that that matters, seeing we're all going to die of skin cancer from the ozone layer being what it is. That hole in the sky over Antarctica's getting bigger and bigger, you know, all the time. Grrr, I hate sun! Rain's nicer. Rain's lovely, all wet and cold and if you're lucky enough you can go out and catch pneumonia in it. Acid rain's best of all.'

'Angie!' Seymour protested in a whisper, because several more passengers were looking, but Angie, enjoying herself enormously, kept on being Morris Carpenter even after the bus stopped at East Merken and they got off. Now she even looked as he imagined Morris Carpenter to be, stomping along with shoulders hunched to her ears. You could almost have sworn she was huddled up in a duffel coat. 'You're a dill, Angie!' he said.

'My name ain't Angie, it's Morris. Morris Mervyn Reginald Carpenter.'

'Get out, no one's called that.'

'Well, he's probably changed his name by deed poll now. What would you know about it, pal? You just watch it. Or watch the pavement, that's more interesting, it's nice and grey and concretey and that way you don't have to look at people, either. People stink. You want to know what really narks me? It's how people say "Have a nice day!" Why should I have a nice day if I don't want to? Next time a taxi driver tells me to have a nice day, I'll slam the door on his fingers.'

'Morris Carpenter wouldn't spend his money on taxis,' Seymour said. 'He'd save it all up and buy cough lollies or books about nuclear war.' Experimentally, he had a stab at being Morris Carpenter. 'Just look at those rotten flowers in the park over there,' he said grouchily. 'Hurts your eyes, doesn't it? I reckon parks should be all asphalt, it looks tidier. Flowers only attract bees and bees sting you.'

'Yeah, let's get out of here,' Angie said. 'Though one place is just as crummy as another. No point in going anywhere, really, might as well stay home all day and pull our duffel coats over our heads.'

But then she came to a halt outside a cream brick building on the edge of the shopping centre and stopped being Morris Carpenter. She stood underneath a pavement tree and tenderly drew out the gift-wrapped china ballet slippers.

'Just who did you buy those nutty things for?' Seymour asked. 'Glad it wasn't me.'

'Cheeky!'

'What on earth would anyone use them for? You couldn't dance in them, you'd get sore feet and glass splinters.'

'They're ornaments, smarty. They're meant to hang up on a dressing-table to stick flowers in, or just to look pretty. I know Lynne's going to love them, even if you're being so rude. That's who we're meeting for lunch. She doesn't even know we're coming, I wanted it to be a terrific surprise. I used to pick her up from ballet class when I lived at home, so it's just like old times . . .'

Three girls came out of the building and stood on the top step, chatting to each other.

'Yoo hoo, Lynne, surprise!' Angela shouted, darting out from behind the tree and running up the steps to hug her sister. 'Oh, it's just *great* to see you! My itty bitty baby sister . . .'

Lynne said quickly over her shoulder to the other girls, 'I have to go, see you both on Thursday,' and came down the steps. She glanced at Seymour briefly when Angie introduced him, but he knew that if she'd walked away then, she would never have recognised him if they'd ever met again. She didn't look much like Angie, apart from having the same large, greenish-blue eyes. Her long brown hair was drawn smoothly back to the nape of her neck and everything about her was controlled and graceful and reserved. She seemed, Seymour thought, a good deal older than fourteen.

'I'm shouting us all out to lunch,' Angie said happily, slipping one arm through Lynne's and the other through Seymour's and setting off jauntily down the footpath, but Lynne removed her arm after a few paces, as though to adjust the shoulder strap of her bag.

'Thanks, Angie, but I can't today,' she said. 'I've got to go home and get stuck into loads of things. We have all this extra school work to do over the holidays, assignments and pre-reading, and I haven't even touched it yet. I've set aside this afternoon specially . . .

'Rats,' said Angie. 'That can wait. You always carry on about homework, you'll have a nervous breakdown if you don't watch out. Come on, I made the effort to trail all the way out here . . . East Merken, what a place to have a ballet school . . . and I haven't seen you for ages and you're coming to lunch with Seymour and me at that Italian place near the station. No excuses.'

'Angie, don't be so bossy. Mum will be expecting me home for lunch.'

'No she won't. Don't you remember, she goes to her ladies tennis thing on Mondays? Come on, Lynne, you need a good feed, anyhow. You're getting that skinny you'll disappear altogether soon.'

Lynne, with a marked lack of enthusiasm, allowed herself to be ushered back to the shopping centre and into the restaurant. Angie wanted to order the most expensive things on the menu, but Lynne protested that she wanted only a glass of lemon squash and a small pizza. While they waited for the food to be brought, Angie produced her gift with a flourish.

'Ta ra!' she cried. 'And wait till you see what's inside! I just happened to notice it in this shop we passed today and I knew you'd love it. So go on, open it up, what are you holding back for! You're getting as prissy as Mum, the way you open parcels.'

Lynne's face didn't register anything very apparent when she unwrapped the little china shoes. Seymour had a suspicion that he detected fleeting exasperation in her eyes, a distaste for the gift, but if that were true, it was immediately masked.

103

'Thanks, it's great, Angie,' she said. 'You shouldn't have spent your money, though. It's not even as though it's my birthday or anything.'

'Why shouldn't I? I like buying you presents, especially ballet things. Just think, when you're famous, you can take those little glass shoes all round the world with you on tours, like a good luck charm. And when I come backstage bursting with pride, I'll tell people it was me who gave them to you.'

'Well, I just hope you won't be wearing those earrings when you come to visit me backstage,' Lynne said lightly.

'Why, what's wrong? I spent ages picking them out and Seymour helped me. Really, don't you like them? What's up with them?'

On display with other sparkling trinkets in the shop, the parrot earrings had seemed cheerfully zany, but now Seymour glanced at the neat little silver studs in Lynne's ears and thought dubiously that perhaps Angela should have chosen something simpler. They were rather too big, rather too gaudy, bobbing about on either side of her face.

'Well, they're not something I would have bought, that's all,' Lynne said. 'But I guess they go with your dress, the colours and everything.'

The food was served, but Lynne ate hardly anything at all. The ice in her lemon squash clinked gently as she stirred it with a plastic straw, and Seymour thought that if a sound could express someone's personality, that would be the sound of Lynne's, the neat, crisp chime of ice cubes against glass.

'Well now,' said Angie. 'What did you learn in class today? Can you do the splits yet?'

'Angie, we certainly don't do the splits in ballet. People always ask that, but you should know better. That, and if it hurts to dance on the tips of your toes. It's so predictable . . . and annoying.'

'Well, I can't remember the proper names of all those steps, even though I learned ballet once, too. Did you know, Seymour, that I learned dancing when I was little? Only for a couple of months, though. I wasn't brilliant at it, like Lynne. She's going to be a famous ballerina one of these days.'

'Angie, shush,' Lynne said, glancing at the nearby tables, but Angie prattled artlessly on, only marginally lowering her voice.

'But you are, you needn't be so modest. Now with me, I was dead hopeless right from the word go. Guess what I did at the first lesson – wet my pants, right there in front of all the other kids! The teacher was so tactful, Miss Bromley or something, did you ever have her, Lynne?'

'No, I already told you before, she wasn't there by the time . . .'

'Anyhow, Miss Bromley just went on demonstrating stuff to the class as though nothing had happened, even with all these little kids staring goggle-eyed at this big puddle in the middle of the floor. Or if they didn't see it in time, they danced right through it and got their little pink slippers soaked. I was so embarrassed, God, I wanted to die! But then a nice kind lady, one of the other kids' mums, came over and mopped it up and took me out to the loo. I never wanted to go back to that class, but Dad made me because of the fees being paid in advance. I had to be in the end of term concert, too, on a proper stage. You should have seen it, talk about a laugh! Do you remember it, Lynne?'

'Angie, how could I? I was only a few months old.'

'Oh yeah, that's right, you would have been. Well, anyway, we had to dance these sort of patterns in lines, being little birds flying or something daggy like that. But I haven't got much sense of direction at the best of times. I blundered right off the stage and got stuck behind some curtains and couldn't find the way out. I've always had a thing about the dark, it was scary, that, sort of smothery and pitch black, like being trapped in a coal mine . . . I didn't go back next term. Different ball game with Lynne, though. She took to it like a duck to water, or maybe I should say a swan to a lake, right from her first lesson. And the way she's going now, we're all so proud of her! She's always being trotted out to the front of the class to show how to do the hard steps, and she gets the jammy parts in concerts . . .'

'Not always,' Lynne said tersely. 'I'm not all that good.'

'Oh, yes you are! Only mind you, Seymour, she nearly didn't make it past her first lesson and it was all my fault . . .'

'Not that old Olga Kozzymunsky story again,' said Lynne. 'Angie, eat your lunch, for heaven's sake!'

'Hang on, Seymour hasn't heard it yet. Well, Lynne was just about killing herself to start ballet when she was five. She used to be always dancing around the living room, even before she had her first lesson. Gee, she used to look cute! So Mum enrolled her, but I did a crummy thing. I was kind of jealous because I'd been so hopeless at ballet, so I used to get Lynne aside and I made up this name and told her that was the name of her new ballet teacher. I'd bung on this threatening accent and say, 'Leedle gurl, I am Madama Olga Kozzymunsky and I am goink to turn you into a beeyootivull dancer! You vill practeese eight hours a day, no excuse, blood blisters vill pop up on your toes, ze cramps, ze womiting . . . ach, never mind, it is nuzzing. I, Madame Olga Tatiana Kozzymunsky, vill turn you into ze most beeyootivull dancer in ze whole vide vorld!'

'Angie . . .'

'And so when poor Lynne turned up for her first lesson after weeks of listening to that, she took one look at the teacher and burst into tears! And that teacher was a really sweet kind little lady, like a sultana bun.'

'Where do you go to school?' Lynne asked Seymour, obviously not wanting to talk about ballet any longer, but also just as clearly not interested in his answer. Seymour murmured something about his proposed new school, knowing that she was only pretending to listen behind her immaculate oval face. His voice stumbled awkwardly. Lynne made him feel all fingers and thumbs, sweatiness and tousled hair.

'Lynne can play the clarinet and flute, too, did you know?' Angie boasted proudly. 'Talk about musical! Oh, it's not fair, here's me always wanted to be musical and I can't even sing in tune.'

'But you can sing okay, Angie,' Seymour said, and she smiled at him over the table, eyes crinkling into happy crescents.

'You reckon? Go on, you're only sucking up!'

'Well, that song you sang the other day was pretty good.'

Angie beamed, then struck a pose and began to sing:

'Like a star in the morning sky,
Your love was there to guide me.
I was weak, too weak to fly,
But you were there, right there beside me . . .
Urging me on, and making me strong . . .
Could hear you saying . . .'

'Angie!' Lynne said crossly, 'People are staring.'
But Angie went on singing, chin propped up on her hands.

'Came back to show you I could fly,
But you had gone without a warning . . .'

'If you don't shut up, that's exactly what *I'll* do!' Lynne hissed. She picked up her bag and shoved the little china shoes inside, almost roughly, although they were so fragile.

'Oops, sorry,' said Angie contritely. 'I forgot you care about what other people think. I know, you can't take me anywhere, always doing embarrassing things in public. Seymour has the same problem, only he's usually too much of a gent to yell at me. Okay, I won't do it again, promise. So, how are the kids at school, Katie, and what's your other mate's name, Teresa?'

'They're all right.'

'And Gillian?'

'Fine.'

'Well . . . I know, anyone want some dessert? How about cheesecake, they have beautiful cheesecake here, not like that horrible yucky stuff you get at supermarkets . . .'

'Nothing more for me, I've definitely got to be going,'

Lynne said. 'There's a whole bunch of things to do. I have to wash my hair for tonight for a start.'

'Why, where are you off to tonight?'

'Oh, just family stuff. We're all going out to dinner and then a show,' said Lynne, pre-occupied with a mirror and comb, even though not one hair was out of place.

'Oh . . . ?' said Angie and there was a short, questioning silence in which Lynne suddenly looked confused and ill-at-ease. She became very busy with the zipper on her bag, which wasn't really stuck and didn't merit all the attention she was giving it.

'It's nothing special, Angie,' she said reluctantly. 'Just something about Dad's work, he got a promotion or something, didn't he tell you? Tonight's do is just a spur of the moment sort of thing. I expect Mum couldn't reach you, seeing you don't have the phone on at your new place.'

'Yes, I guess that's it,' said Angie. 'But I can still come, luckily I haven't got anything else on tonight. Wow, fancy Dad getting another promotion, the Mr Big of the electronics world . . . Listen, where are you all going for dinner? I could meet you there, and I promise I won't wear these earrings. It doesn't matter if you all have seats together at the theatre, either. Maybe they've still got ones on sale at the door. I could . . .'

'I don't know which restaurant,' said Lynne, getting up. 'Dad's boss fixed all that, and I expect they've already booked the table and they can't go mucking it up now with extra people. You won't be missing much, you know how boring it will be, all that computer shop talk. And I don't really know which theatre, though I heard Mum say we were lucky to get the last seats. So there's not much point . . . Oh, look at the time, I've really got to dash now, Angie.'

Seymour noticed that no one, really, had eaten very much. They headed back towards the bus station, but he sensed that Lynne didn't particularly want them to accompany her. She walked ahead very quickly, making no allowance for Angie in her silly shoes.

'I have to take a short cut down National Street,' she said over her shoulder. 'Got to see a schoolfriend on the way, borrow one of her books. So I'll see you around sometime, Angie, thanks for the lunch. Goodbye, Seymour.' She ran across the road with an amber traffic light and waved briefly from the far pavement, then hurried away down a side street, not looking back.

'Isn't she pretty?' Angie said, watching her go. 'You should see her all dressed up in ballet gear, she looks like a princess. I missed her last concert, I could have cried . . . Bet she'll look gorgeous all togged up to go out to dinner tonight, too. It's great having a little kid sister. We've always been so close, you know, right from when she was born. I used to nag Mum to let me babysit, I liked it so much . . .'

She gazed after Lynne, and Seymour looked carefully in the same direction. It was easier to watch Lynne's trim figure disappearing down the side street, much easier than having to meet Angie's eyes, which he now saw were full of sadness. A terrible yearning sadness, like someone who had lost something they'd treasured.

'Come on, what are we hanging round here for?' he said in a Morris Carpenter voice, to divert her. 'Something real nasty might happen and we might miss out on it. Like those dirty big clouds banking up over there, cool change on the way, maybe a thunderstorm. Let's go and stand under shelter and watch all the people get wet! Psst, Angie . . . Carmen Miranda – hey, are you listening?'

'It's just as well they never actually had Morris Carpenter in charge of the weather,' Angie said at last. 'He'd have fixed it up so it rained on purpose for people's weddings and sports days. There's something else I remember about old Morris – he used to have this calendar at school, right, and he'd cross off every day with a big black pencil soon as the last bell went. And he'd mutter, "There, that's one less day to get through!" Cheerful little bloke, wasn't he? One less day to get through . . .'

'There's rain on the way, told you so,' Seymour said. 'We'll get soaked if we just stand around. Come on, Angie, your sister's gone, anyway.'

'Maybe old Morris had a point after all,' said Angie.

Angie,

Thanks a lot for getting me in strife with the neighbours, all that row you made! I thought you were serious about wanting to come off it, needing somewhere to stay and someone to help you through it. What a joke.

I made things clear, Ange, I'm NOT having stuff brought into this flat. You're a creep. You know how dicey it still is for me at this stage of the game.

You probably don't even remember the things you said, the way you carried on. And I DIDN'T dob you in to your mum and dad. It wasn't like that. I couldn't handle the state you were in – what the hell was I supposed to do, ring up that ratbag Rick or someone? Anyhow, your dad guessed soon as he saw you.

Listen, I don't want you round here any more. I mean it. If I lose this flat I don't know where Amy and I could go. I've got too much at stake. Everyone's tried to help you, Angie, but you just use them up. All those times I stuck by you . . . well, I've had enough. I got my act together, why the hell can't you? And I didn't have any family helping me, either. Leave me right out of it from now on.

Judy

God, Angie, this is the hardest letter I ever had to write anyone!

Dear Judy,

I must have missed you on Saturday, knocked for ages and was just about to bust in through your bathroom window and wait (but didn't think I'd better!).

Listen, sorry about all that business last time I was around, didn't mean it to end up heavy like that, honest! Jude, don't give up on me, OK? We've been friends for so long – that letter of yours hurt, you know? I can't believe you really meant it. I know I shouldn't have landed on you out of the blue like that with all my problems and at that hour, but I was pretty desperate. Had nowhere else to go, couldn't think straight. Judy, love, I'm SORRY!

Hey, I've got a terrific little flat now, all self-contained, just about to do it up and everything! You and Amy will have to come round to visit. Amy is a real little doll, you're so lucky, Judy, having a beaut little kid like that. I'm proud of you, the way you got it all together and dropped out of that ratty crowd. I'm doing the same, you wait and see. Judy, don't stop being friends, we've been through a lot together.

Please.


Love from Angie.


P.S. The bundle of clothes I've left on your doorstep, thought you might be able to use them, they don't fit me any more. They are: Doktor Hilde Humpeldink (grey suit, cost a mint, only one of the buttons is missing from the jacket); Lady Arabella Greensleeves (red and green brocadey thing with the gold edging, you might be able to take the skirt up or something); Rodeo Rose (leather fringed skirt and waistcoat, unreal, hey?). Also pink mohair sweater with sequins (some of them have come off, sorry!) and pair of white boots.

The fluffy rabbit is for darling little Amy (to make up for not giving her anything when she was born).

I've got this cute kid who comes round to visit all the time at my new flat. At first I thought he was a bit of a pain. He's about ten, but more like a little old man, honest, you should hear how he fusses over what I eat and that! He's so sweet and I could just about murder his mum and dad, he doesn't say much, but you can tell he has a rough time. He's a lonely kind of kid, it's really sad how shy and lonely he is. If I had a beaut kid like that I'd never let them end up that way. I take him out places and we have a great time, he's real good company believe it or not!

P.S. Gotta rush. Jude, PLEASE don't get Wayne to say you're out when I phone. I heard you talking in the background.

I'm SORRY, OK?

## CHAPTER NINE

'IF ANY OF MY MATES EVER found out I went to the races with an old skinflint like you, I'd never live it down,' Angie said. 'Five dollars in your pocket . . . whoopee doo! Well, I'll just have to tell you what to back and turn you into a millionaire.'

Thelma and his mother considered all forms of betting a ploy of the devil and could quote scripture passages to prove it. Not that it had ever had any effect on his father. Quite a lot of his meagre income had melted away over the years in gambling. Seymour might not have gone if Angie had told him beforehand where she was planning to take him, although he'd known it would be somewhere special by the way she was dressed. Secret Agent, she called it. Secret Agent was black mesh tights, very high patent-leather sandals, a black dress which clung smoothly to her hips then flared out like an urn, and a little saucer-shaped hat with a dotted veil covering her eyes. Seymour thought she looked magnificent, like someone out of a television series.

'I didn't know they had horse racing on week days,'

he said. 'You'd think everyone would be at work.' He'd never been to a race meeting before and kept glancing guiltily over his shoulder in case Thelma or his mother might dart suddenly from the crowd and march him ignobly home.

'Live and learn. It's a good crowd today, I guess a lot of people are still on holidays, same as us. Only no one would even know you're on holidays from that face you've got on. It's a real Morris Carpenter face. You can't play Morris Carpenter at the races, he wouldn't be seen anywhere where people are enjoying themselves. Come on, let's go behind the scenes and give the horses the once over.'

She seemed to know her way around very competently. Seymour had never been closer to a horse than watching the grand parade at a show once, and now hung, mesmerised, gazing over a wire fence at the stalls.

'That one's Maharajah, he's the favourite in Race Three,' Angie said. 'And that little grey is Plumestone, I'm going to put some money on him. People reckon he's had his day, but don't you believe a word. Once he won me a whole month's rent when things got tough, and he can do it again, easy, can't you, fella?'

She chirruped across the rail at the tethered horse and her face was tender, as though she were greeting a much-loved friend. Seymour wasn't surprised that she knew the names of the beautiful horses; it was part of the magic of Angie that she should know things like that. She also seemed to have many acquaintances there, and was constantly waving or nodding to people passing by.

Seymour noticed that they didn't always seem to remember her name correctly. One called her Debbo and another called her Kaye, but when he asked her why, Angie said carelessly, 'Oh, that's nothing, they're just nicknames. You always cop nicknames when you work in racing stables. You didn't know I used to do that, did you? I was a strapper, only the trainer I worked for was a real creep, so I chucked it in. But I really liked working in those stables, except the part about having to get up so early and the boss being such a jerk. You should have seen how I looked when I was taking horses to the races – skin-tight white jodphurs and a pair of gorgeous hand-made boots. They belonged to a famous jockey, those boots, Clive Trelawney, and don't you go telling me you've never ever heard of Clive Trelawney, or I'll thump you! Anyway, those boots hardly had a scratch on them and they were real kid-leather, but he was throwing them out, so I struck it lucky. Some of those top jockeys get very fussy about what they wear. Wow, you could hardly speak to me when I was wearing those boots! Jockeys usually have small feet, see, to match the rest of them, and they fitted me because I've got small feet, too.'

'Have you still got those boots? Can I try them on some time?'

'I don't know where they are now,' Angie said ruefully. 'I moved around a fair bit last year, all over the place, up in Sydney for a while, then back here, stayed in a flat with some mates, I've forgotten half of the places. Some of the things I'd stored at home, but Mum had a cleaning fit and chucked stuff out. You lose a heck of a lot of things when you move around. But if those boots ever turn up again, I'll let you have them to keep. No, honest, I mean it. Then we could go out horse riding one Saturday. There's this terrific place I know out in the hills and it's not just a namby-pamby little riding school, either. You can hire a proper horse and go across country all day. But enough of that now, let's get down to business.'

Before Seymour could come to terms with the unlikely mental picture of himself riding fearlessly across country, she had found a vacant bench under a tree and was busily going through her form guide. Seymour was content to sit for a while, letting the cheerful, highly charged atmosphere lap about him, elated to be part of it and sitting next to Angie in her eye-catching Secret Agent outfit. She was concentrating very hard, her tasselled pencil darting like a dragonfly down the list of names.

'I'm going to put five dollars on Xanadu, for a win,' she said. 'How about you, Seymour. What do you fancy?'

He looked down the list, replete with happiness, for the way she'd said that gave him the illusion that he came knowledgably and often to this fascinating place, and that the little form guide was no more difficult to decipher than a familiar bus time-table. He glanced suavely down the list: Charmaine Waltz, Jewel in the Crown, Black Satin . . .

'They all sound like names for your clothes,' he said. 'Black Satin. Can I put some money on that?'

'Black Satin's fifty to one,' Angie said. 'A real roughie, and trust you to pick that, you dag. But it's your dough. I'll go and place our bets, only don't go splurging more than fifty cents, and you can kiss that goodbye, too. Don't say I didn't warn you, pal.'

She came back with two little slips of stamped paper, and Seymour held his tightly, like a talisman, as Angie hurried him into a stand to watch the race. Black Satin, as though sensing his will vibrating from the crowd, flew around the outside and won by half a length. Any disappointment Angie might have felt at her own lost bet was not evident. She jumped up and down and thumped Seymour joyfully on the back, and when she collected his winnings, he counted the notes speechlessly. Never in his life had he owned so much money!

'Don't get carried away and lose all that on the next race,' she warned him. 'That was just a flash in the pan, beginner's luck. We'll go and look the next lot over really carefully, because there's a chestnut I like, but I want to see if he looks as good now as I remember.'

Seymour could have hung over the rails gazing besottedly at the horses for the rest of the afternoon, but Angie pulled him on, laughing. 'They'll think you're planning to nobble something,' she said. 'You'll get arrested by the stewards and I won't be able to bring you here any more. Warned off racetracks for life before you're even in your teens, that's what'll happen to you. Look, there's that chestnut I had in mind. He's usually pretty smart on this track, though his last run was lousy. Maybe he just had an off day. He looks fighting fit now, don't you reckon? What do you think I should do, bet on him for a place, or go all out for the favourite?'

Seymour leant on the rail next to her, not really understanding her chatter, but highly flattered that she didn't think she had to explain things to him. Suddenly she bounced away, offering no explanation, and when he hurried after her, she was with a nuggety, dour-faced little man.

'Colin . . . I was hoping I might run into you!' she cried.

'Hello, what have you been up to then?' The greeting was friendly enough, but the man continued to walk on as though he had no time to spare.

'How about my old job back, Col?' Angie said. 'Go on, you could put in a word to the boss! I can start any time, tomorrow if you like . . .'

'Sorry, love, there's nothing going.'

'Get away, you're always short-staffed! I ran into Bo the other day in town, she's left. I could have her job, and do it a lot better, too, You know how slack Bo was. Go on, Colin, be nice, have a word with the boss.'

'Listen, Deb, you know as well as I do why you got the chop last time. He gave you every chance but you went and blew it, didn't you? It's your own fault.'

'That's history. I was living way over the other side of town then, and I didn't have any reliable transport,' Angie protested. 'It wasn't my fault I was late a couple of times. Well, all right then, a whole lot of times . . . But I worked bloody hard and you can't say I didn't! I could even live in this time if there's room. And that other business, you know what I mean, what he found in the float . . . that was all a mistake, it had nothing to do with me, honest. I told you . . .'

'No use telling me anything, princess. How about you ask the boss himself and leave me right out of it?' the man said briskly and stepped around her and went on walking, not looking back.

Angie kicked at the fence and glared after him through her little net veil. 'That old grump of a Colin, talk about a sexist pig! He's the foreman at the place where I used to work and I thought there just might be a chance . . . Oh, I should have just spat right in his eye instead of wasting all that charm! I always knew he didn't like girls working there, even though we did a better job than all those other no-hopers they had on! Just because I got sprung, just once for heaven's sake . . . Oh, I'm too mad to bother about this next race, Seymour! It's okay, I'll cool off in a minute, but let's go and get a drink. You hungry?'

Seymour, with all his new wealth, insisted on paying for lunch and felt grown-up and debonair as he carried it back to the table under the trees where Angie sat. He spread out the food, but she ate hardly anything.

'You never eat properly, Angie,' Seymour said. 'You smoke too much, that's why. When you have a baby, you'll have to quit cigarettes altogether. I saw something about that on television one time.'

'Yeah,' Angie said. 'When I have a baby I'll have to turn over a lot of new leaves, just like an encyclopedia, won't I? But who says I'm ever going to have a kid, anyway? That's a very big decision to make, and if there's one thing I absolutely loathe and detest, it's having to make decisions. Besides, there's a whole pile of things you can't do if . . . oh, never mind. And I *am* eating properly, so you can leave off nagging.'

'You only had coffee for breakfast.'

'No I didn't, smartypants. Before you showed up I had a big bowl of All-Bran, can't get any healthier than that, can you? It must have been healthy, it tasted so yuk. Next week I'll get really organised and stock up the fridge and not buy any junk food. And what's more I took some Vitamin C and calcium tablets and stuff this doctor gave me.'

121

'At the North Road place?'

'No, not them. A different doctor, in town. I won't be going back to North Road, we had a sort of row and little Angie got shown the door. It was a lie I told you this morning when you called in for me, that I'd already been out there today and got it over with. North Road's finished and I'm not sorry, either. It wasn't even working, that medicine they were giving me, it's all a big joke. Besides, I don't need any more medicine, I can get along without any. I feel terrific. Just to prove it, maybe tomorrow I'll take you to the beach.'

'I . . . can't swim,' Seymour said.

'What do you mean, you can't swim? Kids can swim, didn't you get taught at school?'

'I failed the test,' he said and felt downcast all over again by that memory. It wasn't fair, once you'd been through humiliation for a certain thing, that should be quite enough, all over and done with. It wasn't fair how shame could rush back and engulf you again, come flooding back into your face . . .

'What about your mum and dad, don't they ever take you to the pool or the beach?'

Seymour shook his head. 'They're busy with their own things,' he said stiffly.

'Oh . . . I'm sorry, I forgot you don't like talking about your folks, do you? Well, all the same, Seymour, there's plenty of things you can learn by yourself without them around. What's to stop you going along to the pool yourself and learning to swim? Not scared of water, are you?'

Scared of making a fool of myself, he thought miserably,

of arms and legs that won't coordinate and the other kids staring and sniggering, teachers getting narky . . . I never want to go through that again, ever.

He looked up and found Angie studying him gently.

'I'll take you to the beach and we'll sort it all out,' she said. 'No worries. We'll find a quiet bit of water and I'll have you swimming in no time. I taught Lynne when she was only four.'

'Probably chucked her in the deep end and rolled around laughing.'

'I never did, you little brat! I don't know why I'm even bothering, but when we go to the beach, it'll be okay, you'll see . . .' She stopped, for someone had placed a hand on her shoulder and was grinning down into her upturned face. Angie didn't return the smile, but the man acted as though she had. He sat on the bench next to her and nodded across at Seymour.

'How are you going, mate?' he asked. Although it was so hot, he wore a handsome leather jacket. Everything about him looked smooth and expensive, particularly the gold link chain around one wrist. He beamed at Seymour over the table, smiling and smiling. Seymour watched him, uncertainly. Something was wrong about that smile – the man's eyes above it were as cold as coins. Angie didn't make any introductions. She shoved her pencil inside her handbag, zipped it shut and started to get up.

'Come on, Seymour, we'd better make a move,' she said, but a hand was placed over hers where it lay on the handbag.

'What's the hurry, Deb?' the man said. 'Haven't seen you around for some time, have I? Now, don't go rushing off on me. What have you been up to? Last time I heard, you and James were racketing all over Sydney taking the town apart.'

'My, you do know everything that's going on, don't you?'

'Well, you know how it is . . . Who's the little play-mate?'

'Seymour,' Angie said curtly. 'He's on school holidays and I'm taking him out for the day.'

'Fancy that, I never imagined you as a babysitter. No, don't go. I'll shout you a drink.'

Seymour looked down at the hand, large and im-placable, as solid as a heavy white china plate. Angie's fingers were scarcely visible and he had the unpleasant sensation of watching a leopard's paw placed over a trapped butterfly. Angie gave a vicious little tug and finally freed her hand, but the man still didn't go away. He held out two dollars to Seymour.

'How about you go over to the canteen and get yourself a drink?' he said affably.

'He's got one already,' Angie said and Seymour felt her shoe nudging his stealthily under the table, signalling him not to go. In embarrassment he pretended to suck on the straw, trying not to gulp air so that the man would know the waxed container was empty.

'Your escort for the day, is he? Bringing you any luck, any big wins?'

'We're getting there.'

'You want to try that Bruce O'Neill filly in race six. Long odds, but you never know, you might end up with something. Say four-hundred-and-fifty dollars or thereabouts.'

'I can pick my own horses.'

'Four-hundred-and-fifty dollars would be a tidy little sum to win. Come in handy for paying off outstanding debts, wouldn't it?'

'If anyone owes anyone else that much, I'm sure they'll settle eventually,' Angie said. 'They always do, don't they?'

'But they never took so long about it before. Still, you know me, I'm easy going. I'll even give out more credit if it's needed, if people want to pop around this evening and pay something off their accounts. After they've delivered their little chums back to the sandbox.'

Angie took out her mirror and applied lipstick, adjusted the veil on her hat, and although she looked composed enough, like any girl tidying herself after lunch, Seymour saw that her hands were shaking a little.

'I won't be dropping in this evening or any other time,' she said. 'I don't need to. I've got my act together now, going really well, you ask anyone.'

'Whatever you say.'

'This time's different. Jas and me, we're making a real go of it.'

'From what I heard, young James won't be around for the next couple of years, will he?'

'Look, I haven't got time to sit around talking to you,' Angie said coldly. 'I made it clear enough last time. Some people are pretty dense about messages. I won't be dropping in, but you don't have to get in a stew about . . . I'll send it to you through Rick or Gayle or someone, okay?'

She stood up and the man remained seated, tapping his white fingers lazily on the table top, smiling up at her. Seymour was suddenly filled with animosity so powerful it catapulted him to his feet and around to Angie's side. He took her hand and tugged her away. The man seemed to have no claim to be part of the sparkling blue and gold day. He was like a mismatched piece of jigsaw puzzle that didn't belong with the clean animal smell of horses, the turf like a stretch of sea water enclosed by white rails, the sun gilding the passing women in their charming summer clothes.

'Don't forget, Debbie,' the man spoke softly after them. 'I don't like my books being out of order.'

'Angie, who was that guy?' Seymour whispered, but Angie didn't reply and didn't seem to be listening to him, either. She seemed to be away in some other world of her own, with her eyes functioning automatically to steer her around people and obstacles, but he knew that she wasn't really seeing them. After a few attempts at conversation, Seymour shut up and just sat in the stand while she went off periodically to place bets, waited for her to emerge from her silence and be cheerful, scatty, generous Angie again, the best companion he'd ever known. But that didn't happen until far into the afternoon, and he had no way of knowing if she'd won or lost money, for she didn't tell him. The betting, somehow, had ceased to be for pleasure and had become a grimly serious affair with her, strong enough to block out his presence. He waited patiently, and then, although there was still one more race scheduled, she said it was time to leave.

'Let's get out of here before all the traffic,' she said, smiling brightly at him as though the past two hours hadn't even happened. 'You've got no idea what this place is like when everyone's trying to leave at once and all the trams are packed. Have a nice day, did you, love?'

'Yes, it was great,' said Seymour, for although the shadow of that man lurked unpleasantly about in his mind, he still had most of his original winnings. 'Thanks for letting me come to the races with you. It was beaut.'

'That's okay,' Angie said. 'Know what? I'm glad you wandered in off the alley that morning! You're really good company, Seymour. I'd have gone nuts in that flat not knowing what to do with myself and Jas being . . . We've had a fantastic time, haven't we, all the places we've gone to?'

'Better than Morris Carpenter ever had.'

'Morris Carpenter? He's finished and done with, died of gloom disease, it finally caught up with him. Let's play something different, let's play Mangel Wurzel. What, you've never heard of Mangel Wurzel? Well, it sort of goes like this: Eee, lad, wha thee been oop to then, haring off to sinful gambling places with that there young hussy from down t'lane? Don't you deny it, now, our Seth and our Gertie seen thee with they own two eye!'

Seymour grinned. Angie had altered her face so she looked like a pernickety old village woman. He could almost see floury hands and an apron.

'Such goings on!' scolded Angie. 'Never took place when old squire were oop t' big house, I can tell thee! Ecky thoomp! A body can't sleep peaceful with things cooming to this pass, a nice young lad like you, pockets stuffed with wicked gambling money, belly full of apple cider . . Thee ought b'rights be out in fields a digging oop them there turnips!'

She played Mangel Wurzel all the way on the tram

out to Victoria Road, but as they walked up the alley, a brisk little wind scurried along the dark flagstones and Angie shivered suddenly in her thin dress.

'More rain and thunder on the way. I hate these cool changes,' she said. 'You can feel the air getting colder; ugh, it's like something creeping up on you in the dark! Well, here's your gate and you're home with fifteen minutes to spare. Honest, I don't understand why you flap so much about always getting home before that Thelma. She can't eat you. I'm like Cinderella's godmother, always got to get you home before you turn into a pumpkin. Or a mangel wurzel. Ouch, tottering around in these shoes all day . . . hang on while I take them off. My poor feet, what I'd like to do is fall into a bath filled up with that scented bubble stuff and stay there for about a hundred years! Stay there for ever and never come out . . .'

Seymour climbed the locked gate and gazed down at her. 'If you're tired you could have an early night, Angie,' he said.

'Oh, could I now?'

'Well, you never look after yourself, so someone has to nag. After you have dinner, a proper one and not three cups of coffee and a million cigarettes, you ought to go straight to bed.'

'Can't,' said Angie. 'I'm going in to get changed into Senorita Rosita. You haven't seen Senorita Rosita yet, have you? It's red and black ruffles with a big red rose on one shoulder. Then I've got to go out again, all the way back into town and I won't be home till late. So, yah.'

Seymour could tell she was tired by the blurred lines

of her face and the way she stood slumped against the fence, shoes dangling by their straps from one hand. Even the feather on the jaunty little hat had drifted from its anchorage to curl limply by her cheek.

'You're nuts!' he said. 'Who says you've got to go out? You shouldn't . . .'

'Anyone would think you were my elderly uncle, the way you carry on,' she scoffed, and attempted a skittish dance on the flagstones, holding out her skirt with one hand, but her bare feet on the stones traced meaningless, fuzzy patterns. 'I'm not a bit tired. I'm going into town to rage, and if you were a bit older, I'd maybe take you with me. No, I don't mean that! I wouldn't ever take you where I'm going, it's not a very refined place. Your aunty Thelma wouldn't approve, for a start.'

'She's not my aunty, I keep telling you. I reckon you're crazy to go out again. You'll maybe get that flu thing back all over again. There's going to be a big thunderstorm, you can feel it building up, just like yesterday. You'll get soaking wet, Angie . . .'

'Morris Carpenter would be pleased.'

'. . . seeing you never wear that raincoat, what's its name again?'

'Agatha Christie,' Angie said. 'Wouldn't be seen dead in that, but I can't chuck it out, either, seeing my mum gave it to me only last Christmas. I'll be fine, I can look after myself. You'd better go in now, buster. I'm glad you liked the races and the horses and one day when I've made a million you can come and live with me in my mansion in Gresham Avenue and we'll go to the races every week. You can wear a white carnation in your buttonhole and we'll turn up there in a big silver Rolls, how about that?'

'Wow, only I'd better drive, seeing what happened to your other car,' he said. 'I don't fancy getting tied up in power lines, I'd sooner dig mangel wurzels all day. Don't you stay out too late, Angie. See you tomorrow.'

She waved and turned to go away up the alley, and to Seymour, still watching from the gate, she seemed to be reeling with tiredness, each footstep a conscious effort. 'Hey, Angie,' he called anxiously. 'Listen, I just thought of something. You know how you always see me home down the alleyway? Well, if you go out tonight and get home late – and this is a rough area, Thelma says so – well, who's going to see *you* home safely down the alley in the dark?'

'That's not a problem, Seymour,' Angie said lightly. 'That's never any problem.'

I won't go round there and see him!
The baby hang on to that, getting a house with Jas hang
on to that, my baby

I WON'T go round there and see him! I won't go round
there and
Make a fresh start I can do it what if S. ever found out
I can do it I can do it Jas wish you were here make
Mum and Dad proud of me hang in there I can do it
I don't need

I WON'T GO ROUND THERE
Take it five minutes at a time Angie take it easy now
lots of other people get there Judy did my baby think
of my baby wonder what colour hair it will have OH
GOD IN HEAVEN I CAN'T STAND THIS ONE
SECOND LONGER

Negative thinking take it easy Angie sure you can ring
up Jude or someone hop under the shower wash hair
go for a walk scrub kitchen floor keep busy I won't go
round there
Lynne David think of Lynne and David think of flowers
my flower shop I can do it yes I can yes

I won't go round
Today is the beginning of the rest of my life
Today is the beginning of the rest of my life
Today is the beginning of the rest of my
I won't . . .

## CHAPTER TEN

THELMA SPRAINED HER
shoulder and took a couple of days from work to rest
it, and Seymour realised just how small the house was
with two people cooped there, neither of them able to
avoid the other for very long. Although she didn't seem
to enjoy his company, she berated him when he stayed
in his room for long periods. 'Is that what you do when
I'm at work, stay in your room and sulk?' she scolded,
more tetchy than ever with the pain from her shoulder.
'You're making heavy weather of this situation, young
man.'

'But I wasn't . . .'

'I can't help it if you're not allowed out on your own.
You know very well why you can't go out. Your father's
not to be trusted. He'd be whisking you off to Queensland,
using you as a lever to try to get poor Marie to go back
to him, we all know the pattern. Sulking won't help
things. When all's said and done, it's only temporary
until your mother moves to the new place.'

So he joined her reluctantly in the living room on

the clinging vinyl chairs where he knocked ornaments from small tables with his restless elbows. He pretended an interest in the boring midday movies she watched, but his presence pleased her no more than his retreat to the back room. Every time he shuffled his feet she sighed with pointed forbearance. While she watched television or read the paper he leafed, limp with heat and boredom, through all the books in the shelves. Whenever possible, he slipped out the back and stood peering through the gate slot across the alley at Angie's place, even though he didn't catch one glimpse of her.

He felt aggrieved about that. Wasn't she even slightly concerned by his absence? He thought forlornly that she could at least come to his back gate and call over it, make sure that all was well with him. If you were truly friends with someone, you'd worry if they didn't show up. Perhaps it was all a phoney act on her part, that big sister stuff. He glared across the alleyway, but nothing stirred beyond Angie's open gate. There was a white dress on the clothesline there. It hung, motionless in the heat, as dry as timber, but no one came to fetch it in, and it was still there the next day.

Finally one morning, Thelma moved her shoulder cautiously and decided it was improved enough to return to work. Seymour pulled a secret face of relief. He didn't think he could have borne one more day of her austere company.

As soon as she left he hurried across the alleyway and knocked on Angie's door, but although it was ajar, she didn't answer. He pushed it open and shook his head at the horrendous state everything was in. Angie's attitude towards housework was always lackadaisical, but

133

now it looked as though a storm had careered through the room, snatching things from their places and dumping them on top of other things already on the floor. Angie was asleep, lying fully dressed on top of the blankets, and while he automatically put the jug on to make coffee, she suddenly plunged into some alarming dream situation which made her thresh about and cry out.

Seymour patted her gently until she opened her eyes. 'Hey, it's okay, don't be scared,' he said. 'It was only a bad dream. I get them like that sometimes.'

But Angie kept trembling, wrapping her arms around her as though to contain the shaking, and her face was a bewildered mask of smeared cosmetics. Mascara lay in caked black smudges across her cheeks. Seymour dampened a towel under the tap but she just looked at it blankly when he held it out. He dabbed clumsily at her face.

'There,' he said. 'Now you'll feel better. Have you got the flu back again, Angie? Well, I did warn you. If you don't look after yourself properly, you can't expect . . .'

That's if she ever did have it in the first place . . . The thought rolled about in his mind, heavy as marble.

To his embarrassment, she burst into tears, groping for tissues in a box that proved to be empty and flinging the box across the room at a wall. He stood by helplessly until she stopped crying, just as abruptly as she'd begun. She sniffed once or twice like a child and dug her knuckles into her eyes, then she lit a cigarette.

'Don't take any notice of me,' she said shakily. 'I'm just feeling a bit down, that's all. I'll be okay. I'll get up in a minute and have a shower and get dressed, only there's no hurry, I don't have to go anywhere in particular. I don't have to go out to North Road any more, did I tell you? Not today or tomorrow or the day after that, either. I got kicked off their rotten useless program . . .'

'Yes, you told me. Here, Angie, have some coffee.'

She drank half a cup, then huddled back against the bedhead, the tears drying on her face and her eyelids drooping then snapping open again. She plucked at the sheet, making a little hole in a patch of frayed threads. Seymour began to talk, not wanting her to fall back into that wild place where she'd been in her sleep. He told her about Thelma's sprained shoulder and the movies they'd watched and how tedious the past days had been.

'So that's why I couldn't come over to visit,' he finished, feeling guilty, even though it hadn't been his fault. She'd looked so white after that day at the races, so tired. He should have nagged a bit more and somehow prevented her from going out again that night. Maybe then she wouldn't be in this state, wouldn't be so . . . peculiar. He made a grab for the ashtray and just managed to stop ash from spilling all over the blanket. Everything she did seemed uncoordinated, even her languid responses to his chatter didn't somehow mesh. He wished she'd wake up properly, then they could go out somewhere, out into the clear morning which sparkled like wine held in a glass up to the sun. But she just continued to sit there, hunched up, gazing at the hole she was making in the sheet.

'Angie, are you listening to me?' he demanded, exasperated, and she finally made an effort and dragged her gaze upwards.

'So,' she said. 'You had a good day at the races yesterday? Really did you enjoy it, or were you only pretending?'

'It wasn't yesterday we went to the races, Angie. It was Wednesday, don't you remember? Yesterday I couldn't come over, or the day before that. Thelma was at home. I haven't been over for . . .'

'This place is past a joke,' she said fretfully. 'In ten minutes I'm going to get up and springclean, wash the curtains, vacuum everything. It is a mess, isn't it?'

'Well, I guess you could say that. Ash all over the place doesn't help, either. You aren't going to have another cigarette, are you? Come on, you just put one out.'

'Bossyboots,' she said. 'You're like this teacher I had at school, what was her name, Miss Rydges . . . Rydell . . . oh, I can't even remember her dumb name! God, I hate it when I can't remember things.'

'Don't try and change the subject. Now's a good time as any to give up smoking, while you don't feel well. You said at the races you were going to give up without fail, cross your heart. What happened to that?'

'Don't nag! Tomorrow, maybe.'

'It's in the papers all the time, how it makes people get lung cancer. If you give up, it adds ten years to your life. Ten whole years you can buy new earrings and wacky looking clothes. Don't you want all that extra time?'

'What?'

'Don't you want ten extra years to live?'

'Not particularly.'

Seymour stared at her.

'The idea doesn't grab me all that much,' Angie said.

136

'You know, sometimes I just want to go . . . home. Wherever that is. Home before dark . . .'

'Your place?' Seymour asked, puzzled. 'I thought you didn't like it there. You said your mum and dad pick on you all the time.'

'I didn't mean . . . oh, forget it. Get lost!'

'Hey, Angie, what's the matter?'

For she'd suddenly rolled sideways, clutching her stomach and moaning raggedly to herself. Beads of sweat sprang up across her forehead, but when he touched her hand, it was as cold as snow.

'Go away!' she whispered savagely. 'Go on, nick off, go away and leave me alone! You little pest, I never even asked you to . . .'

'Angie!' he pleaded. 'Listen, I reckon I should go and tell someone. You might have appendicitis, you get a pain in the gut when you have appendicitis . . . Should I go and get your landlady?'

'That old bitch! She'd kick me out. Don't you dare let her in here stickybeaking . . . Oh God, I can't stand this! Find Juliet for me, who took her? Where's Juliet?' She snatched up a battered rag doll from the floor and held it tightly, rocking to and fro. 'Juliet, got her for my fifth birthday,' she whispered. 'Been with me through thick and thin. All the times I've moved, Seymour, you just wouldn't credit the other things I . . . lost. My charm bracelet Dad gave me, that was worth a mint, I got a new gold charm every Christmas, you know, he'd pick them out specially, and I went and . . . I feel so ashamed. And Grandma's little pearl earrings, real pearls . . . can't remember where, Brisbane, I think. There was a photograph frame, all silver . . . Oh, God in heaven, all the things people gave me, and I just . . . just . . .'

'Well, you didn't lose Juliet,' Seymour said, looking at the doll with astonishment and wondering how she could be so attached to it. It had a melancholy white cloth face and wasn't particularly attractive, with dingy, frayed clothes needing a good wash. It smelled, but when he tried to take it away, Angie slapped out at him and started to cry again.

'Okay,' he said hastily. 'It's just I wouldn't hold it close up to your face like that. That doll kind of pongs, Angie.'

'I don't care! You don't know what she means to me, been with me through . . . Dad used to tell me bedtime stories, see, when I was little and he'd make up ones about Juliet, what she did every night when the whole house was sleeping. She used to dance round the garden in the moonlight in her little shoes . . . I believed it. I thought she was real, and she started school the same day I did . . . Oh, hell, I can't bear this! I've got some tablets somewhere to take, not that they help . . .' She pushed herself up on one elbow and scrabbled about in the drawer of the bedside table. She found a little packet and shakily peeled away the foil backing, swallowing tablets with the cold dregs of the coffee.

'All that many?' Seymour demanded, alarmed. 'What is it, aspirin? I don't think you should be taking so many all at once. Thelma gets tension headaches from where she works, but she never takes more than . . .'

'Oh, belt up, it's only prescription stuff I got from this doctor in Upton Street. That might be a lot for some people but I'm used to them, been on them for ages. It's funny, I thought I had more, a whole new packet . . . maybe I used them up last night. Oh, God, I feel so crook! I'm sorry, love, I was going to take you out some place today, wasn't I? Going to take you to the races, you'll like it there . . . Don't go away. I'm scared . . . stay and keep me company, keep me comforty I feel so cold keep getting these cramps remember when I showed you the beautiful . . .'

She was suddenly asleep, drawn down into slumber like a pebble into deep water, not surfacing. Seymour had never seen anyone fall asleep so quickly, and suddenly feeling very frightened and alone, he lifted her eyelids, not even knowing what he was looking for. He recalled vaguely that you could tell if people had lapsed into unconsciousness by the state of their pupils. Angie's were huge and dark, almost engulfing their rims of pale iris, and they stared at him, unmoving. He spread a blanket over her, tucked her cold hands under it and ran across the alley to Thelma's house.

He fumbled through the phone directory to Easterbrook, found a Merken number and dialled. After a long time, while his mouth went biscuit-dry with nervousness, for he'd made scarcely more than half-a-dozen phone calls in his life, someone answered, but it wasn't Angie's mother. It was Lynne, sounding breathless and slightly annoyed, as though she'd just been on her way out and had been obliged to run back to answer the phone.

'It's me, Seymour, I live near Angie. You know, we all had lunch together that day . . .'

'Yes?' Lynne said, after a pause.

'Well, I've just been over to see her and she looks real crook,' he babbled. Crook, he thought. I should have said ill, sick. Lynne doesn't use words like crook, she talks posh . . . 'Angie's sick,' he went on miserably. 'She should see a doctor.'

'Well, she's been sick other times and she's managed,' Lynne said. 'She's got plenty of friends who help her out. Did she tell you to ring me?'

'No, but I didn't know who else. She took some tablets but they didn't seem to help. She was all sort of peculiar, her voice sounded funny. One minute there she was talking to me and the next minute she just . . . well, sort of flaked out.'

There was another silence from Lynne's end of the line.

'Is your mum home?' Seymour asked.

'No, she isn't,' Lynne said brusquely. 'She's gone out for the day and I can't get in touch with her. I was just about to go out, too. Look, couldn't you . . . There's some doctor Angie goes to on and off, only I can't remember his name or where he is. Couldn't you wake Angie up and find out his number? If you rang him up, maybe he'd make a home visit.'

'I can't wake Angie up, I already tried,' Seymour said, resentment rising at her slowness to help and at her apparent lack of sympathy. 'And before she fell asleep like that, she was rolling around clutching her stomach as though she's got appendicitis. Rubbing her arms and legs, too. And she'd been . . . well, sort of sick. Before I went there, I guess. It was on the floor next to the bed, only she didn't seem to notice. I didn't like to say anything, embarrass her . . .'

'All right, then,' Lynne said angrily. 'I suppose I'll just have to come over and see what's going on. Wait a

**140**

minute, I don't even have her new address. She moves
so often Mum doesn't write it down in the Teledex any
more. You'll have to tell me how to get there, just a
moment while I get a pen.'

When he finished directions and she hung up, the
thud of the receiver was like a sharp rebuke, as though
she meant that he should no longer concern himself
about the matter. It was as though she'd actually tacked
such a message on to everything else she'd said, that
he should mind his own business, but he went back across
the alley all the same.

Angie hadn't moved, but the rag doll had fallen to
the floor. Seymour picked it up and tucked it back into
her arms, feeling foolish, but not knowing what else to
do. He cleared a chair and sat next to the bed and
waited, and it was a very long time before he heard
footsteps outside. He leaped up to open the door, but
Lynne gazed at him with such unfriendliness that he
felt he'd done something horribly uncouth and wrong
in summoning her at all. She went straight past him
to the bed and stood looking down, but nothing in her
face mirrored his own concern.

She bent to shake Angie by the shoulder. 'Wake up
and tell me what the trouble is,' she said. 'No, don't
you dare go back to sleep, I didn't come all this way
and miss my lesson just to . . . Oh, it's hopeless, the
same old story, and I can't do anything for her. You
don't have to look like that, she's not unconscious,
she's . . . I'll just have to ring Dad at work. Oh, this
place, it's such a pig sty, you couldn't bring a doctor
in here without cringing from embarrassment.'

'You can use our phone if you like,' Seymour said,

shrinking from the distaste in Lynne's eyes, as ashamed of the untidy room as though he were somehow responsible. 'I live just over the alley.'

Lynne nodded ungraciously and followed him across to the green gate and he suffered more embarrassment explaining that it was kept locked and she'd have to climb over. In those smart, freshly laundered clothes, she wasn't really the sort of person you could expect to scramble over a gate. There was no softness about her, apparently no kindness at all. He pitied Angie for having such an uncaring sister and as he led the way to the phone, he tried to convey by his stiff back the way he felt.

Lynne dialled a number and, while waiting, glanced about at Thelma's possessions. Her eyes flickered over the cheap cane telephone table, the padded stool next to it, the garish oval flower prints Thelma had pinned to the wall. Then she looked coolly at Seymour and he found himself retreating, full of resentment, to the living room while she made the call. How dare she cast those critical eyes over Thelma's genteel poverty? How could she be so unemotional and detached when Angie, her own sister, was obviously so ill? And the way she was speaking into the phone, asking for her father as though she were just ringing up to discuss something as ordinary as being picked up from one of her old ballet classes! She had the kind of voice Thelma and his mother referred to as 'nicely spoken', but Seymour didn't think it was an apt description. Not if it meant only words clipped out so that you practically heard each distinct cold syllable.

'I'd like to speak to Mr Easterbrook, please. This is

Lynne, his daughter, calling, and it's fairly important. Thank you, yes, I'll wait till he's off the other line.'

He could hear the sound of her breathing, the impatient tap of her fingernails drumming on the cane table. He knew it wasn't polite to listen to someone else's phone conversation, but in that tiny cramped house there was nowhere else to go, unless he were to open the front door and stand casually on the veranda staring down Victoria Road. That would look stupid, and besides, Thelma had forbidden him to open the front door. He couldn't go back into the kitchen, either. The hall was so narrow that when anyone used the phone, the passageway was effectively blocked. He stayed where he was in the living room and made a pretence of not listening.

'Dad? Angie's gone right off the top again, yes, the usual, what do I do? Mum's not home . . . I'm not ringing from home, anyhow. Some kid phoned me, that little boy Mum told you about, the one Angie brought out to lunch that time. I don't know anything about him, he just lives across from her . . . You should see the terrible dump she's living in, it's gross, nearly as bad as that boarding house . . . No, I didn't see any, but I didn't make a point of looking, did I? Dad, I don't want to . . . I *won't* stay with her! Mum said I shouldn't have to ever . . . Oh, *all right*, then! Well, it's a sort of flat in an alleyway. Yes, the alley's wide enough to get the car down, but you be quick, okay? I don't want to be with her on my own, having to talk to her if she wakes up, you know what it's like . . . It's always so . . . ugly!'

She passed on all the detailed street directions Seymour

had given her earlier, then slammed the phone down quite hard. The little brass ornaments which Thelma dusted so assiduously every day chimed against one another in protest. Seymour went back into the hall, hardly daring to look at her, but she said with composure, 'Here's thirty cents to cover the phone call.'

'You don't have to,' he said politely, though Thelma had a small slotted cannister on the cane table firmly labelled 'Phone Money'. Lynne, however, had slipped the coins in already and picked up her neat leather overarm bag. She went out through the back door, not waiting for him, but Seymour followed.

'You don't have to come back there again,' she said, halfway over the gate. 'Thanks for letting us know. I should have said that before, shouldn't I? Well, thanks, anyhow. Angela will be fine, my father's coming from work and he shouldn't be long. He'll take care of everything.'

'I was . . . I should . . . maybe I should stay with Angie, too, till he gets here,' Seymour stammered, so unaccustomed to defying people that the words felt as brittle as dead leaves in his mouth. He couldn't even meet her eyes, this cool, poised person who had more claim to Angie than he had. But he didn't like to think of those eyes raking scornfully over the sad disorder of Angie's room, and Angie lying helpless in bed, unable to defend herself against that intrusion. Angie needed someone else to be there during the waiting, a friend . . .

'I said you don't have to,' Lynne snapped. 'You're not even related to her. It's silly, you know, a little kid your age hanging around with someone grown up. Mum said so. She was very surprised your mother or aunt or whoever it is lets you roam about all over the place with a twenty year old. Specially someone like Angela.'

'What do you mean, someone like Angie?' Seymour said indignantly, and the indignation bolstered some feeble reserve of courage. 'Why are you being so rotten to her? Your mum was, too, the day we went out there, not even looking at her birthday present properly . . . She just shoved it away in that cupboard, hardly even bothered to look at it! What's wrong with your family? Not even asking her to that dinner you all went to . . . You all charged off to the theatre and you didn't even ask her along, she was hurt about that . . . Angie's feeling crook . . . sick. I bet you won't even put the blanket over her if she's knocked it off again! She's got the flu really bad, she gets it all the time . . .'

Please let Lynne say it's the flu, he thought desperately.

'You don't know anything about it, so you can just go back inside your house and stay there!' Lynne said. 'You keep right away from Angie, you're only wasting your time trying to help her and be nice to her. How dare you say we never . . . for your information, Dad's got to leave an important meeting and take her to Rankin House! And that makes the third time since . . .'

'Rankin House? Is that a hospital? How long will she have to stay in there?'

Please, please say it's the flu . . .

'She never ever stays there more than a couple of days . . . Oh, you mind your own business!'

Her voice was as final as a slammed door and he stood wretchedly in Thelma's garden, listening to her footsteps across the alley. After a while, all defiance gone and replaced by sadness, he peered out through the slot above the padlock. He could see the grey flagstones and the open gate of Angie's yard. He waited for a long time, chilled in spite of the blazing sun, and eventually a car turned into the alley. Seymour blinked. He'd expected Angie's father to be a stern, forbidding sort of person, but the man who got out and hurried in through the opposite gate was too ordinary to be anyone's idea of an ogre. Mr Easterbrook came out just as quickly, carrying Angie wrapped up in a blanket. Lynne held the rear door of the car open while Angie was placed inside, and then she and her father got in and the car edged back into the traffic of the main road.

Seymour watched it all and raged silently, 'All her family, they're so rotten and stuck up, you've only got to look at them! They don't give a stuff about Angie. That Lynne, she can hardly wait to get off to her old ballet class, doesn't give a damn, you only have to look at her! Him, too . . . the way he just dumped her in the back of his rotten car like she was a sack or something . . .'

But he knew that actually, that wasn't the truth of it at all. He'd caught a glimpse of their faces as they'd carried Angie out to the car, and what he'd witnessed there was a kind of raw and hopeless grief.

pram, cot, singlets, bassinet, baby bath, nappies, maternity clothes, talc, playpen, bunny rugs, pusher, bouncinette, bibs, jumpsuits, plastic pants, booties, nappy pins, baby album, ceiling mobile - cow jumping over the moon, night light - teddy bear one, shawl, carry basket, high chair, mosquito net, little woollies, rattle,

NAMES:
David, James Jamie Jimmy, Aaron, Troy, Stuart, Andrew, Patrick, Seymour.
  Melissa, Lynne, Jeanette, Juliet, Judith, Kylie, Samantha, Kirsty, Lyneve, Chantelle, Fleur.

Supporting Parents benefit or whatever it's called?
Part time job somewhere, Jude might babysit for me?
Put name down for emergency state housing flat?
Share house with other single mums?
Get help from Mum and Dad? (NO!)

Get help from Jas's sister? (NO WAY!)

Adoption? (NO NO NO!)

Get rid of it . . .

Oh God!

## CHAPTER ELEVEN

SEYMOUR'S DAYS SEEMED TO have no focus now and worry about Angie filled his whole mind and soul. It even drove him to answer Thelma back the next evening at dinner. She was watching his unenthusiastic attempts at eating and reprimanded him with, 'You shouldn't waste good food like that. You're moping again, young man, that's what you're up to. I know it hasn't been much fun for you here, but it was all we could do under the circumstances. Your mother . . .'

'Well, if you really want to know what I think, she's always making a stupid big drama out of everything,' Seymour snapped, weary of it all. 'It's like cloak and dagger stuff, this hiding out . . . It wasn't even needed. She just likes all the fuss.'

Thelma looked at him, astonished, as though a piece of her furniture had spoken.

'Like a TV soapie, the way she carries on,' Seymour said, not knowing the effect his outburst had caused, for he was looking with distaste at the plate holding the unappetising heavy food Thelma always served, no matter what the temperature. 'Dad's not really like what she makes out, he's not a criminal. What's he ever done that's so awful, anyway, except going round the pubs? If people got off his back he might manage a bit better. You can't blame him for wanting to see me now and then, either. She should have let me stay at that caravan park till school went back. I didn't mind it. One night it was nice – everyone had a barbecue down by the river and Dad got hold of someone's guitar. I never heard him play before, never even knew he could! She never asked me if I wanted to stay on there, just told me to pack my things up. It wasn't . . . fair. He gets lonely, like everyone else . . .'

'As he deserves to be!' Thelma said tartly. 'I don't know how you can sit there and defend him after all the trouble he's caused! That shiftless . . . Why, he never ever got a proper home together for you all, not to mention Marie having to work all these years to meet the bills. If anyone deserves your support, young man, it's your poor mother.'

'Well, anyhow, he didn't come charging down Victoria Road and take off with me,' Seymour muttered. 'I never even thought he would. It was just Mum, carrying on . . . It was just a waste, a pain in the neck, all this. Three-and-a-half weeks of sticking around inside and not being allowed out . . .' He stopped, guiltily conscious that he hadn't really been doing anything of the sort, and added hastily, 'Sorry, I didn't mean it like that. Mum kept saying she didn't know what else she would have done if you hadn't let me stay here. I hope I wasn't too much trouble.'

'Well, I can understand it hasn't been easy for you,' Thelma said unexpectedly. 'I told Marie at the time it wasn't the ideal solution, this house being so small and not much space out the back. Children don't like being cooped up and you've been very good about it, on the whole. Heaven knows, I'm not the ideal companion when I get home from work, either. Too set in my ways. I'm not used to having kids about the place. It's not much longer, though, only till the weekend, then you'll be moving out to Carrucan with your mother.'

Seymour gaped at her, for it was the first expression of sympathy he'd heard since coming there to stay. Obviously it paid to rock the boat a little and not always absorb things that happened to you without complaint. He wasn't sure if it were worth the effort, though. His heart was racing from that uncharacteristic ourburst.

'Well, I suppose I should consult your mother first, but I don't really think it would do any harm if you went out occasionally during the day,' Thelma added briskly. 'Just down to the shops, or there's a public swimming pool on the other side of the park. Only be careful, mind. Keep a sharp eye out and if you see your dad hanging around, you get yourself back here quickly and phone me at work. Here's a dollar if you want to go swimming tomorrow.'

Seymour was pleased and grateful, though he still had all the money he'd won at the races carefully hidden in the back room. 'I can't take this,' he protested, embarrassed. 'You're still paying off your house, Mum told me. It'll be okay when we move out to Carrucan, anyhow. I might get a paper round.'

A paper round, he thought wryly, remembering the last time he'd tried that. It had lasted exactly three days, and he'd been so bluffed by the territorial dogs in that area he'd made some pathetic excuse to the newsagency about his bike having been stolen.

Thelma insisted that he take the money and he reflected that he'd never been so rich in his life. Only now it seemed an empty thing without much joy. Angie wasn't there. He couldn't run across the alleyway and say casually, 'Come on, Angie, get your earrings on, I'm taking us both out today!' He thought bleakly of the empty flat opposite.

'Thelma, have you ever heard of a hospital called Rankin House?' he asked, clearing the table while she had a cup of tea, and making his voice as offhand as possible.

'Rankin House,' she said absently, reading the letters to the editor in the paper. It was the first page she always turned to, but it didn't seem to give her much satisfaction. She was given to reading the letters aloud, making scathing comments about the views of each correspondent. 'Yes, I know where that is, it's quite close to the city. You can see it on the left when you go through Knudsen railway station. A red-brick building and it's got a notice board over the gate, private hospital, I think.'

'Just an ordinary hospital?'

Please let it be . . .

'Goodness, Seymour, I don't know. I've never taken all that much notice, it's just a place you see from the train. Why do you want to know about it?'

He tried to think of reasons. School holiday project on hospitals, he thought wildly, knowing that wouldn't do at all, since he'd left his last school and was to start a new one. 'Nothing in particular,' he said evasively, for she was peering at him over the top of her reading glasses. 'I mean, I heard someone mention it once, just the name . . . I thought it might be a . . . a school or . . . maybe a prison or something like that . . .'

'Then why did you ask if it was a hospital?' she said and then cried with exasperation, 'Really, Seymour, that's a sloppy way to stack the dishes! Rinse them under the cold tap first as I showed you.'

Next morning after she'd gone to work, he collected the key from under the flowerpot and crept into Angie's flat, thankful that its door couldn't be seen from the main house. He was afraid of that formidable landlady, and although he had a speech prepared – 'Angie's been in hospital for a few days. With flu. But she's coming home soon, so I've just dropped in to clean out the fridge for her.' – he was sure he'd muff it if she just happened to be around and demanded to know what he was doing there. He wasn't planning to tackle the fridge only – he meant to clean up the whole place as a welcome-home surprise. He remembered the mess on his last visit and had come prepared for hours of hard labour, but when he shut the door behind him and turned around, he found that someone had already been in and done it. The bed was neatly made and all the things on the sink had been washed and set to drain. The linoleum under his feet shone, its pattern now visible, and there was a tang of pine-scented cleaner in the air.

Seymour's first reaction was disappointment. He'd spent all the previous evening planning how he was going to spring-clean the flat and have it glowing to welcome

Angie home. A couple of days, Lynne had said. Well, in that couple of days someone, the landlady he supposed, had got there before him. Perhaps Mrs Easterbrook had phoned and told her about Angie being in hospital and she'd had a twinge of conscience for being so heavy about the rent. Angie wouldn't be at all pleased about her messing around in here. However, there was one small job he could do. He went importantly to the fridge with a cloth he'd brought with him, soaked in vanilla essence. Thelma did that whenever she cleaned her fridge, to make it smell fresh.

But someone had already defrosted and scrubbed out Angie's fridge, and forgotten to switch it back on. Seymour attended to that and closed its door, so it would be ready for storing food. Somehow he was going to have to find the courage to go all the way down the alley to the shopping centre, risk facing that gang of local kids, and buy a stock of food. Healthy, nourishing food, like oatmeal porridge and fruit and wholemeal bread, using his race money. It was the last thing he could do for Angie before he left with his mother tomorrow afternoon.

The bathroom recess was spotless, too, with the grouting between the tiles scrubbed, and the shower mat hanging bone dry on the rail. There was no cleaning left to do there, but in the far section a pile of Angie's clothes lay on the bed. It looked as though someone had begun to straighten out the wardrobe and hadn't had time to finish. Well, that was one other thing he could do for her – re-hang all her clothes neatly in the wardrobe.

He worked deftly and methodically, taking wire hangers

from a bundle on the floor, and became so engrossed in creating order from chaos that he didn't hear someone walking into the back yard and opening the door. Sunlight flooded in across the freshly washed linoleum and he looked up, startled, to find Lynne staring at him.

'How did you get in here?' she demanded aggressively. 'Why's the door unlocked?'

'The spare key . . . Angie keeps one under the flowerpot in the garden. I'm not doing anything, just hanging all this lot up for her . . . tidying up . . .' His voice trailed away in embarrassment, he felt incredibly foolish standing there clutching an armful of gauze flounces. It was some outfit of Angie's he'd never seen her wear, some kind of glittering party dress, though knowing Angie, he guessed she would have worn it any time of the day she felt like it. He quickly put the frivolous dress on the hanger inside the wardrobe and stood shuffling his feet. Lynne's expression made him feel as though he were an intruder, prying into someone else's possessions when he had no right to.

'Well, you've been wasting your time,' Lynne said. 'They've got to be packed away. We slaved all yesterday afternoon to get this place cleaned and we're just finishing off now. Mum dropped me off because she's got some urgent shopping to do, but she'll be back in an hour and I can't work and chat at the same time. I'm sorry, but you'd better go now, okay? Oh God, where do I start? All these awful clothes . . . Didn't you hear me, Seymour? Go on, run along back to your place! You shouldn't even be here. Does Angie know you just pop in and out when she's not home?'

'Of course I don't!' Seymour said furiously. 'I only

came over to tidy things up for when she gets back. I was going to put milk and stuff in the fridge. You said she only ever stays a couple of days in . . .'

'Well, she's not coming back here. This time she's made other plans. And you'd better give me that spare key, too, before I forget about it. They have to be returned to the lady who owns this place. Look, if you don't mind, I have to get all this stuff packed and ready to go in the car when Mum comes. There's really nothing for you to do.'

The dismissal was as clear as though she'd typed it out and handed it to him in an envelope, but Seymour stood his ground and watched as she began to take the garments from the wardrobe. All his careful, painstaking work had been in vain. Lynne just crammed things impatiently into a large plastic bag as though she wanted to get the whole business over and done with.

'Angie likes it here,' he said distantly. 'She was going to get some rolls of wallpaper from this discount shop she knows about and do it all up. She's got the colour scheme all worked out and everything. And she was going to ask if she could dig up the flower bed and plant climbing roses and stuff there. How do you know she's not planning to come back? Did she tell you herself?'

'Oh, for goodness' sake, Seymour, you don't know the first thing about it! Angie's obviously been trotting out all her usual fantasies, and you've just been dumb enough to believe them. She's definitely not coming back here, she's going away interstate, leaving tonight. Dad's picking her up from Rankin House when he finishes work and driving her to the airport. I wish you'd go home. Can't you take a hint? You're holding me up, standing there

155

chattering about things you don't even understand. Oh, I've had this cleaning up! Honestly, all the tacky rubbish Angie manages to collect . . .' She tried unsuccessfully to wedge several pairs of shoes into the overladen bag, swearing irately under her breath. Seymour stared at her. Lynne was normally so cool and composed, it was rather unnerving to discover that she not only knew bad words, but would actually use them.

'And there's no sign of her suitcase,' she finished bitterly. 'Lovely beige leather, with an overnight bag to match. We got it for her on her last birthday. What on earth are you doing? There's no use looking under the bed and up on the wardrobe for it! Probably sold it, didn't she, like she does with any expensive present anyone gives her. Only she never ever says "sold", it's always "lost". When I think how David and I put all our holiday savings towards that birthday present . . .'

'There's some more plastic bags on the sink,' Seymour said. 'You could pack the rest of the things in those.' He went to fetch them, battling to keep all expression from his face and to empty his mind of any feeling. He'd had plenty of experience with saying goodbye to people and places before, he reminded himself. You didn't let yourself become too involved, that was the secret. Angie was just a person he'd met by chance during this particular holiday break, and in a couple of months he'd probably forget all about her, wouldn't even be able to remember the outline of her face or how her voice had sounded. A troubled person, someone it was best to forget, anyway. It was pointless to be hanging around here where he obviously wasn't wanted. Futile to watch Lynne handle all those possessions so unkindly, stuffing them away out of sight as though she found each one repugnant.

'I guess I'd better be going,' he said woodenly and moved to the door.

'Hang on a minute . . . if you really want to help, you could clear out the things from the kitchen cupboard,' Lynne said, and her voice was less sharp, as though she regretted biting his head off like that and was ashamed of it. Seymour hesitated, then turned back and silently began to remove everything from the shelves and stack them on the sink. There weren't many items – a few mismatched plates, the wobbly saucepan, a chipped teapot. 'They're not really worthwhile keeping,' Lynne said. 'I don't suppose the next person who moves in here would want them. The whole lot could go out in the rubbish bin.'

'This, too? This looks too good to throw out,' Seymour said, finding a small cup and saucer of fine china right at the back. He wiped them clean with a cloth and they shone with resurrected bright colour, waterlilies and dragonflies emerging vividly from a layer of dust. They looked unused, as though Angie had perhaps valued them too much to risk in everyday use. He carried them carefully over to the bed. 'Funny Angie having something like this, all in one piece,' he said. 'She was always breaking things. She told me that's why she bought cheap stuff at op shops for the kitchen, so it wouldn't matter much if . . . what's the matter?'

He stared in astonishment, finding it hard to believe that Lynne's self-contained face could so suddenly be flooded with emotion. She took the cup and saucer from his hands and turned them about gently, tracing the bright patterns, obviously fumbling towards some almost forgotten memory.

'Fancy Angie keeping . . . The shop near the school, that's where I bought it . . .'

'Did you give it to her her?'

'She used to walk me to school and we'd pass this particular shop and this was in the window. Years ago, when she was still at home, she must have only been about fourteen. She thought it was so pretty, so I saved up all my pocket money in secret. I kept worrying that someone else would buy it before I could. That was the year before it all started, really, before everything went so . . . She was so nice up to then, I wanted to give her something special, because as well as being my big sister, she was my best friend, too. And then it all changed, there was this really awful crowd of kids she got in with . . . She used to tell lies all the time about where she'd been . . . Oh, poor Mum and Dad, the things she put them through!'

With an effort she regained control, making her face impassive again, and returned briskly to the task of packing.

'We're storing all this stuff of hers at home as usual,' she said tonelessly. 'Until the next time. I've lost count of the number of times . . . Oh, why does she buy these terrible clothes? She can't possibly want this thing!' She held up the silver lace shirt Angie had been wearing the first time Seymour had met her, and it seemed now to have no connection with the reality of everyday living. It seemed garishly out of context, like something that belonged to a theatre stage. 'I'd better not throw it out,' Lynne muttered. 'She remembers all the clothes she owns, sometimes months later just when you think she's forgotten all about them.' Her glance kept returning to the fragile little cup and saucer which she'd placed so softly in the centre of the bed, and suddenly she stopped what she was doing and sat down and covered her face with her hands.

Her emotion raged as wildly as a flame. Even though it was soon brought under control, Seymour was shaken by its intensity. His mother's sadness always manifested itself as long rambling vocal complaints, needing only patience from the onlooker. He didn't know how to help someone seared by such a profound grief as Lynne's and stood by helplessly.

'I don't usually cry about it,' she said, angrily dabbing at her eyes. 'It's so useless. Goodness, if I blubbed about it every time, I'd never get anything else done. It's been going on for so damned long. You can't cry that long over someone, no matter how much you love them . . . how much you used to love them, can you? Five whole years, that's how long she's been on drugs . . .'

The bats were released from the compartments of his mind as though someone had treacherously released a spring-catch. They assailed his whole being with their black fluttering. All the elaborate pretences he'd so carefully built were no longer any use, and he stood, stricken, confronting the finality of Lynne putting all his troubled suspicions into ugly words. Drugs . . . Angie . . . that's how things were with Angie.

'Sometimes I feel as though I hate her,' Lynne said dully. 'The things she's done to our family, the terrible times she's put us all through. All those promises . . . she goes off to some rehab place and then after a couple of weeks she nicks off and we don't hear from her for months. A place called Lakeview, that's where she's off to tonight, though I don't even know why they're bothering to take her back. Three weeks she lasted there last time.'

'Maybe . . . this time will be different,' Seymour said wretchedly, and his voice struggled thickly through layers of angry, bewildered sadness. Angie . . . All those lies she'd told! All that advice she'd given him – she was one to talk! It was as though he'd been marooned on a desert island, and someone had come along and rescued him in a little boat. Promised to take him to safety. Only that person proved to know nothing about navigation, had taken him instead into rough wild seas . . .

'I'm certainly not getting my hopes up,' Lynne said. 'I don't even know why she's promised to go back there. I just don't trust her and her promises. One minute she was yelling at us saying she wouldn't, then she broke down and started wailing that she didn't have any choice . . . Oh God, it was so pathetic, you should have seen how relieved poor Mum and Dad looked last night when she said she'd give it another try. They looked so happy, believing it all. Angie's going to stay at Lakeview six months like a good little girl and someone up there will wave a magic wand and she'll come back completely cured . . . They only believe it because they've got to have something to hang on to. I certainly don't any more. She's had five years to get her act together. Sometimes I think the best thing is to forget I ever did have a sister.'

She picked up the pretty cup and saucer and wrapped

them carefully in layers of clothing, placing them deep inside the plastic bag.

'Well, if you've given up on her, why are you going to all that trouble?' Seymour demanded. 'Why don't you just dump that thing out in the rubbish can?'

'Because it's something from when she was different, before all this started. We had some lovely times together when she walked me to school. She made up all these games. There was a big steep hill we had to go up and I used to get tired and start complaining, you know how little kids do. But she'd pretend we were astronauts exploring another planet and if we reached the top of the hill we'd get to meet all these silvery people, they'd have silver eyes and hair . . . And she'd give all my clothes and her clothes names, that's another thing she'd do. Apfel Strudel, Little Miss Muffet – that was blue and white checked gingham . . . I remember looking up at her and feeling so proud, she always looked so pretty people kept turning around to notice her.'

'They still do.'

'Not for the same reasons.'

'What's that supposed to mean?'

'Angie . . . she doesn't live there any more, it's like someone came and stole her away . . .'

'She still is nice! You talk about her all the time as though she's . . . dead.'

'Well, sometimes that's exactly how it feels. There's a lot of things you don't know about her, the things she does to get money. And her horrible friends . . . One of them broke into our house and stole a whole lot of stuff, and she knew all about it. Probably told him when we'd be out and the best time to do it.'

'Come on, Angie wouldn't . . .'

'Oh, Seymour, for heaven's sake, you don't know anything about it! She can and does when she gets desperate enough! Anyhow, that man's in gaol now for something else he did, and it's a pity they don't lock him up for good. Jas got her on drugs in the first place! Listen, you just forget about Angie, she's not worth bothering about. I'm going in to return the keys now, and you'd better go back home. There's nothing left to do here, it's all finished.'

She shooed him to the door and he caught one last glimpse of the empty room, but there didn't seem to be much presence of Angie left in it. It was just a vacant, rather bleak structure in someone's back yard, waiting for the next tenant.

He went out into the alley, dazed with unhappiness, but as he crossed to his own back gate, a fragment of colour drew his attention. It was Angie's old rag doll, stuffed into a rubbish bin awaiting collection. He drew it out and went uncertainly back into the yard, wondering if he should leave it on top of the plastic bag full of clothes. But Mrs Easterbrook and Lynne, who obviously didn't understand its importance, would probably only throw it out again. He stood holding it by one floppy arm and heard Angie's voice whispering in his mind, 'Juliet, been with me through thick and thin . . . Oh God, the things I've lost . . .'

He knew that he must bear responsibility for it. Post it on to her, if he could find out the address of that Lakeview place, and include some sort of message, though he didn't know what he could possible say –

Get well, Angie. Stay there and get well. Stay there

forever if it takes that long, only get well . . . Angie, please get well . . .

The only trouble was that such things were impossible to say in a letter.

Oh I wish, how I wish
That I had a little house!
With a mat for the cat
And a holey for the mouse;
And a clock going tock
In the corner of the room,
And a kettle, and a cupboard,
And a thick new broom!

## CHAPTER TWELVE

RANKIN HOUSE WAS LISTED
in the Hospitals section of the telephone directory, and
there was something else added after its name –
Alcoholism and Drug Treatment Centre. Seymour slowly
dialled the number and asked if he could speak to
Angela.

'I'm sorry, it's not possible for you to call patients
on this line or to leave messages,' an impersonal voice
told him. 'Hospital visiting hours are between three-thirty
and five each afternoon.'

He hung up and went and tidied himself in the
bathroom, although that was just to fritter time, for
he was neat enough already. A painfully neat kid, not
really equipped to deal with this new burden sitting so
heavily on his shoulders, looked back at him. He frowned
at that reflected, timorous face.

It's nothing to do with me, anyhow, he thought with
anguish. Lynne said so! Angie got herself into this mess
and they've all tried to help her and there's nothing
more anyone can do. She's just a liar! All those rotten

lies she told me . . . I don't have to go and see her.
I should watch that crummy old TV set all afternoon,
forget about her . . .

It was tempting. He winced at the thought of having
to go to a strange, alarming place and ask for Angela.
Ask to see a drug addict, a junkie – wasn't that what
they called them? Perhaps she would be in bed, in one
of those intimidating, high white hospital beds, with other
people in the same room, other . . . junkies. And how
would he manage to talk to her, how could he possibly
bridge this huge furrow that had ploughed its way through
their friendship? Maybe she wouldn't even want him
to see her in a place like that. A memory of a photograph
stirred in his mind, something he'd once seen in a
magazine, shock tactics to warn kids about drugs. It had
shown a girl, eyes black-rimmed, skin white as death,
slumped on a squalid concrete floor. Fleetingly, he saw
Angie's face superimposed on the photograph . . .

He spent an agonised half hour, decided to leave the
house at once and visit her and get it over with, then
finding dozens of tame excuses to avoid it. For instance,
he could just write to her casually instead. Could phone
the Easterbrooks and ask for the Lakeview address, giving
some reason – Angie had lent him a book and he wanted
to send it on, or she'd forgotten to return a pen of
his and he wanted it back – but none of those excuses
sounded convincing. And besides, there was the rag doll,
for which he had taken responsibility. He glared at it
morosely, knowing that he couldn't take something like
that on public transport, it would have to be disguised.
He wrapped it in a striped tablecloth of Thelma's, the
first thing to hand, and shoved the whole lot into a

166

plastic bag. Then he climbed over the back fence into the alley.

'Strewth, Angie,' he thought with despair, gazing down the dangerous length of the alleyway, buffeted by all his fears. 'The things I do for you . . .'

No one was about, and he plunged into that dark river, floundering towards the tram-stop end, but before he could reach it, two kids suddenly walked in from the entrance. They halted when they saw him, whispering together, and the sunlight blazing behind made them seem like malevolent science-fiction figures. Seymour's footsteps grew leaden and trembled to a stop. He glanced behind at the long stretch of flagstones leading back to the other main road, and knew that was a useless route of escape. The distance was too far. His own gate was too far away, so was Angie's, and besides, she wasn't there to protect him. After a moment he trudged on hopelessly, his throat tight with fear, until he was close enough to see their faces. Alert faces, full of latent mischief. They didn't move, but stood casually in the centre of the alley, positioned so that he couldn't walk between them. Seymour came to a halt, he couldn't do otherwise.

'Well, look who's here. If it isn't that kid we saw the other day, the one in the park with the grandpa hanky,' one of them said. 'Where's he off to, then?'

'Sunday School,' said the other boy, grinning. 'Boy Scout Jamboree.'

Seymour tried to keep his face neutral, but to his disgust found it slackening into a glib, ingratiating smile. A smirk, you could call it, nothing else. Something he'd read once crossed his mind, about the behaviour of wolves in a pack. How, if one were threatened by a more dominant wolf, it would lie fawning on its back, offering its neck to the threatening teeth, and its action would somehow defuse the situation. That's what he was doing now, and he felt sickened by his cowardice, but couldn't help it. Wearing the ghastly stiff grin, he tried to step around the boy by the right-hand fence, but that space suddenly vanished, so quickly it was hard to tell if it had actually been there at all.

'I'm just . . . just doing messages,' he stuttered. 'Had to go into town for someone . . .'

His fear was as evident as scent, he could almost smell it in his own nostrils. Panicking, he tried to force a way through the two boys, but again the space moved and ceased to exist. Someone laughed – an unpleasant sound, not like laughter at all.

'What you got in that bag? Let's have a look . . .'

He jerked it back instinctively, his action springing from shame at being caught carrying a doll and the urgent need to get it to Angie before she left. Maybe the last thing he could ever do for her.

'Pongy washing, bet that's what it is,' one of the boys jeered. 'Off to the laundromat with his spare hankies . . .'

Under snatching, relentless fingers, one of the plastic bag handles broke, revealing a section of the tablecloth, garishly striped in red and blue bands. Seymour found his voice, battled to hold it steady, chatty even, and kept his fingers tightly hooked in the other handle. 'This?' he said. 'Well, it's . . .' Oh God, what had Angie called them, that day at the races? 'Jockey's silks,' he said with forced swagger. 'You know, those jackets jockeys wear in horse races.' Trying to sound like a myriad of other kids in playgrounds displaying prized possessions . . . 'My dad gave me this, my uncle brought this back from . . .' And always himself on the fringe, not included, suffered to be part of the audience.

'They belong to Clive Trelawney,' he said in a rush. 'My uncle. Got to get them to him right away, he's riding in a big race this afternoon.'

'Clive Trelawney's your uncle? Get out!'

'Yeah, he is. He's riding a horse called Plumestone, fifth race on the program. This jacket, I mean these silks, they've just been dry-cleaned. You know how it is, all those top jockeys are dead fussy about the way they look on the track. I'd take it out and let you have a proper look, only they're folded a special way . . . Still, I guess you can watch the race on telly if you're interested.'

All the time he was walking, step by small ragged step, heart thumping, towards the alley entrance. At least they'd let the other handle go, and he looped it around his wrist with a show of casual importance . . .

'My old man's always placing bets down at the shop,' one of the kids said conversationally. 'He won five-hundred dollars once on the Quadrella.'

'Well, you tell him to watch out for a horse called Black Satin. A real roughie, but it can sometimes win you a whole month's rent. Specially if my uncle's riding it. See you round some time . . .'

He was scrambling up on to the tram, glancing back at the kids, and they didn't look threatening at all, now. One of them even gave him a half wave. Outwitted, he thought, with pleased surprise. You don't always have to roll over and offer up your throat, there are other ways you can get out of things. Other ways where you come out the winner.

The elation of being a winner stayed with him while he got off the tram at the railway station and bought a ticket to Knudsen. He stopped at a flower stall, thinking that he should buy something for Angie. You always took flowers to people in hospital, even if the Rankin House place wasn't really a proper one. But the stall flowers were unspectacular bunches in identical wrappings, as though they'd all been processed in some factory. The only thing out of the ordinary was a sheath of pale stems dotted with small silvery moons. Each disc felt like silk stretched delicately over framework.

'That stuff's called honesty,' the assistant said. 'Present for someone, is it, love? People buy it to put in dried-flower arrangements, but it looks nice on its own, too. It's expensive, though, we don't often have it in stock.'

On the way to Knudsen station, he thought dubiously that, expensive or not, he might have made a mistake about the choice of flowers. They didn't look very exciting, nestled in their tissue wrapping, just a handful of brittle little circles the colour of milk coffee. But there was no time to worry about that now, he had to find a red-brick building on the left-hand side as described by Thelma. It was easily visible from the train, but when he got off, he became lost in a maze of narrow, illogical streets while trying to find the entrance. Angie and her hospitals, he thought irritably. Why can't she ever pick one in a place that's easy to get to!

After trudging around a complete block, he found the entrance at last, with a large sign above the gate saying

'Rankin House'. The sign didn't carry the extra information that had been in the phone book, and he was glad of that, grateful that Angie's trouble wasn't advertised to all the passing traffic in the street. Now, he thought, all I have to do is walk into the reception hall, that should be easy enough for Clive Trelawney's nephew. It's visiting hours, they said so on the phone. All I have to do is ask for her . . . nothing to it . . .

But when he forced himself to go through the gate, he was unexpectedly amongst a crowd of people in a small barren garden. He hovered, stricken by bashfulness. Many of them were visitors, he could see that by the bunches of flowers being handed over, and there were kids, too, amongst the visitors, so he didn't really look out of place. But at first it was difficult to tell which ones were patients. He'd been prepared for dressing-gowns and hospital wards and nurses in the background. Disorientated, he stood looking around and suddenly located Angie without having to ask anyone. She was sitting by herself under a tree on the far side of the garden, looking very subdued and small, like a lamp turned down low. Even her clothes were lack-lustre – washed out old jeans and a shirt faded to the colour of water. Her hair hung in slack tendrils around her lowered face, and she was playing listlessly with a long stem of ivy, winding it around her fingers.

Seymour went across, skirting the groups of other people, and knelt down beside her. He was taken aback by the tremendous start she gave, as though she hadn't heard his footsteps across the lawn, as though his sudden appearance had jerked her back from some other dimension. She nearly jumped out of her skin, he thought, bemused, and saw just how pale and delicate her skin was, close up. Almost too fragile to contain such a complicated and vulnerable thing as a human being.

'Anyone would think I was a ghost,' he said. 'Hi, Angie, just thought I'd come and visit you.'

'How did you know where I was?' There was no welcome in her voice. It sounded flat and tired, but underneath the flatness lurked something that could, he sensed, flare into anger directed at him for coming. He'd made a mistake. He should have stayed away.

'Your sister said Rankin House . . .'

'Lynne? She's been talking to you?' The something glinted like a blade in the sunlight.

'Not really what you'd call talking,' Seymour said quickly. 'It was only on that day when you . . . got so sick and they had to pick you up in the car. Rankin House was sort of mentioned casually.'

'Casually, eh? Sort of casually enough for you to know the address.'

'Hey, calm down, Angie. Lynne didn't even say the address. There's that notice board you can see from the train, I just thought it might be the same place. So I dropped in to visit you, that's all. Only you're not exactly giving me the red carpet treatment, are you? Talk about grouchy – it's like . . . like visiting Morris Carpenter!'

Angie relaxed visibly and a shadow of her old effervescent smile crossed her face. 'Okay, I'm sorry. It's just I don't like people talking about me behind my back. I thought . . . oh, never mind. Anyhow, you'd feel grouchy, too, in a dump like this. It's a proper hole, this place, you just wouldn't believe it. The rooms are like shoeboxes, that's why everyone sits out here getting

172

sunstroke. You go crazy in those little shoebox rooms – I was starting to feel like an Adidas sneaker. The matron, my God, you should get an eyeful of the matron! She eats live yabbies for breakfast . . . So, what have you been up to? I've missed you heaps, you know. And guess what, pal, my flu's nearly gone.'

Seymour didn't say anything. He looked away from her contrived effort to sparkle, glanced at the other patients, seeing faces superimposed upon a photograph.

'Soon be out of here, though,' Angie said gaily. 'This evening, as a matter of fact.'

'Yes, I know. You're going to . . .'

'Countdown to freedom, I've been marking off the seconds. Wow, I can hardly wait to get home, back to my flat.'

'The flat? But that's . . .'

'What's the matter? You look as though someone just donged you over the head with a crowbar.'

'Angie, your mum packed all your stuff away and they cleaned up your flat. They gave the keys back to the lady who owns it. There's nothing . . . Hey, Angie, you're joking, aren't you? Lynne said you'd be going to a place called . . .'

The ivy stem snapped like wire. Angie cast it away and began to tear at another, binding it around her fingers. 'I remember now, they did mention they'd be cleaning up the flat,' she said. 'I tend to let things get in a right old mess and Mum's such a . . . It'll be nice to find everything all tidied up for a change. There must be some mistake about the keys, though, some mix up. Doesn't matter. That old dragon lady will be glad to see me back – no one else would want to rent a tiny place like that. Not for what she's asking. I should have . . . I was going to discharge myself this morning, only I have to wait around for the results of some dumb blood test they . . . Let's talk about something else, huh? I know, how about tomorrow morning you come over to the flat and we'll go to . . . Oh, there's dozens of places we haven't been to yet! There's ice skating . . .'

'All your things are at your mum's house,' Seymour said hoarsely. 'All your clothes, everything. Lynne reckoned you knew about it. She said . . .'

'Ladybird, ladybird, fly away home. Your house is on fire and your children all gone,' chanted Angie, aping his troubled voice with a degree of malice he didn't know she possessed. 'Listen, Seymour, you stay out of this! Lynne and her casual conversation . . . she's been at you, hasn't she? Telling you lies. You don't want to believe anything she tells you, she's just plain jealous of me having a flat of my own and being independent . . .'

'Angie, you sort of promised them you'd go to Lakeview . . .'

'Lakeview, where the hell's that? I don't know any place called that! Mum just popped in to clean my flat and that's all there is to it! Got it all ready for me to go back to, because I was sick . . . I asked her . . . I'm *not* going to . . . They all seem to think . . . Hey, come on, let's change the subject. You know what I thought of buying for my flat? One of those gorgeous big prints, they cover a whole wall. I saw this fabulous one like a forest scene – tree trunks and light coming down in a shaft . . . It will look great up on that wall behind my dressing-table.'

'People ought to keep promises.'

'Let's change the subject!' Angie said with taut desperation. 'Visitors are supposed to talk about nice things in hospital. I've been sick, really sick, you know. I got a kind of pleurisy on top of that flu. Pleurisy's serious, people can even . . . If you've just come here to hassle and nag me like everyone else, Seymour, talk me into . . . Oh, forget it! I don't feel like visitors anyway! Why don't you just nick off home?'

Seymour remembered the gift he'd brought her and handed it over in defeated silence.

'Oh, a present – it's lovely,' Angie cried. 'You're sweet, bringing me a present. I've always loved this stuff, too, though I can't remember what it's called. It'll come in really handy. Did I tell you I'm thinking of getting stuck into making things and selling them at craft markets? Little boxes with pine-cone lids, fabric picture frames, you know the sort of thing. I could use this – what's it called . . . fennel? No, that's not right. Oh, God, I hate it when I can't remember things! You might be able to help me out at those craft markets, be my assistant. We'd have fun . . .'

'I go back to school next week. I'm moving tomorrow with my mum to the new place.'

'Where is it? I never knew you were moving . . .'

'Honest, Angie, you and your rotten memory,' Seymour said, thinking how far away that unknown suburb had looked on the map when his mother had pointed it out to him. 'I already told you about Carrucan a million times.'

'Well, I'm no good at names and dates and stuff. Here, write down your new address on this paper the dried flowers were wrapped up in, then I won't have any excuse for forgetting next time. Carrucan – that's way out past the airforce base somewhere, isn't it? Never mind, no worries. I'll be able to buy another car with what I make from my craft market sales. Something really jazzy, a little four-wheel drive, maybe. I'll whizz out to Carrucan and pick you up and we'll go on safaris. Oh, don't I wish I had that car right now! I'd be out that gate and away, right to the edge of the map and off!'

Seymour glanced around at the other patients. Most of them were young, like Angie. He studied the faces of the visitors. They chattered brightly, ribbons of cheerful sound festooning the air like bunting, but it somehow sounded false and laboured. The eyes in the bright faces of the visitors didn't somehow link with the chatter. Sad, worried eyes . . . everywhere he looked.

'You're always talking about . . . about nicking off to places,' he said jerkily.

'So what if I am? Any law against it? What's the matter with you, biting my head off like that?'

'It's true. It's the way you always carry on. I bet even if you did have that car, the nurses wouldn't let you take off in it. Your hands are all shaky. You couldn't . . .'

'There's nothing wrong with me!' Angie said rapidly. 'Just a little bout of flu, that's all it was. Why, I could have stayed home in the flat and got better all by myself. It was just everyone fussing – you know what parents are like. I'm feeling fantastic now, really I am. I still look pretty. I look terrific, don't I? Come on, Seymour, you're my pal, don't you reckon I look terrific?'

'About as terrific as everyone else in here,' Seymour

said, carefully not looking at the other patients and their visitors.

'Them? What's that supposed to mean? I don't look a bit like them! They're all absolute no-hopers, that lot – that skinny guy over there, he's in and out of this place like a yoyo! And Samantha, that twit with the frizzed up hair, she's nothing but a . . . Some friend you are, saying . . . Specially when I never even asked you to barge in here and poke your nose into my affairs, you little twerp! Bothering someone in hospital . . . Go away! Go on, nick off!'

'Okay,' Seymour said. 'No point in hanging around if you just jump down my throat every time I say anything. I'll go, then.'

'Good! I'm certainly not stopping you!'

He gathered the small stems of dried flowers together. Angie with her restless, agitated hands had messed them up and they no longer looked like a neat, shop-assembled gift. Seymour wrapped them again in the tissue paper.

'That's a lovely present,' Angie said distractedly. 'Did I thank you for it? I'll be able to use it in dried-flower arrangements when I get my florist shop. My goodness, all this fuss about a little attack of flu and pleurisy, you're just as bad as my parents . . . I've forgotten what this dry stuff's called – it's not fennel, is it? I'm well enough to get up and walk right out of . . . Bracken, that's not it, either . . . Oh, I wish I would remember the names of things!'

'It's called honesty,' Seymour said and suddenly felt very tired, too tired to bother about the bouquet. He dumped it next to her, not caring that the fragile moons scattered fragments of themselves into the dusty grass.

'That's what it's called – honesty. Geeze, Angie, you go rattling on about bronchitis and flu, but we both know what . . . The flat, that's all over and done with, there's nothing left there now. You can't go back there.'

'There are other places! I've got friends . . .'

'They all want you to go to that Lakeview place, you know they do. It's some kind of home where they help you get off . . . drugs, isn't it? You promised them you'd go there. Your dad's coming in to pick you up.'

'I won't be here when he does! They can't make me go if I don't want to! It'll just be like all those other times I tried – a waste . . . it never ever works out . . .'

'Maybe you never give it a chance to.'

'Don't you dare start preaching at me! I've got enough to worry about. Got to find somewhere else to . . . Samantha reckons it shows now. They don't like renting flats to people with kids, neighbours complaining . . . poor little baby . . . poor little thing. Oh, God, what a mess! I wish now I'd just . . . just . . .'

Seymour suddenly thought of the baby he'd seen all those years ago, remembered clear eyes gazing peacefully into his face. He felt sick with distress.

'Any kid of yours is going to have a great time, isn't it?' he said stiffly, getting to his feet. 'A real lovely time it's going to have! You falling asleep every time you come down with . . . with flu, and it can just bawl its head off. You probably won't even hear, Angie. Falling out of its cot and you won't hear that, either! You reckon you like little kids – all those times we went out and you saw a pram, you'd stop and have a look and go all clucky. Talk about a big act!'

'I'm good with kids, you ask anyone! I'd never . . .'

'You'll be falling asleep with a cigarette burning the place down. It's okay, I'm going. I don't want to stay here any more and talk to you. You make promises and don't . . . They booked you into Lakeview and your dad bought the plane ticket. They're all trying to help you . . . All you've got to do is bloody go there wherever it is and stay for a while!'

'Get lost, Seymour!'

People were turning to look. An older woman with a tired, concerned face hesitated and half rose from a bench, but he didn't care. For the first time in his life he didn't much care if people turned to gape at him if he were causing ripples. He felt angry enough to wish that the ripples would surge into a whirlpool large and powerful enough to swallow up the whole mess, take Angie away, cover up the frightened eyes in the garden, swirl away the whole sad, terrible business.

'Babies can smile really early, did you know that?' he said bitterly. 'Yours probably won't have much to grin about, though. Where's it going to grow up, Angie? You haven't even got anywhere for it to live. Oh, I forgot, there's that posh house on Gresham Avenue, isn't there? Or maybe in the back room of your florist shop . . .'

'You rotten little creep! I never asked you to come in here and lecture me! You get the hell out of here – I didn't want to see you, even! I never even . . . *liked* you!'

'Well, I don't like you much, either, Angie,' Seymour said and turned to go, but something was dragging at his wrist. He tore at the knotted handle of the plastic bag and let it fall into Angie's lap. 'Here,' he said. 'You might as well have it. Little girls like playing with dolls.'

179

He went away, not looking back, not able to look back, and walked numbly through the intricate streets to the railway station. The air shimmered with heat. Waiting for the train, he found himself blinking and screwing up his eyelids, for the sky seemed to be filled mysteriously with white-hot, silver flecks. They flickered like miniature rain and dampened the backs of his hands when he touched his eyes.

No little winged horse, he thought, looking up into the sky, trapped in the numbess that wasn't, after all, free from pain. He blinked the illusion of silver rain from his eyes. There would never be any little winged horse plunging splendidly from the sky to land at your feet and carry you away from things not to be borne. That was something you had to learn to do all by yourself.

*Hi, Seymour!*

*Guess you'd never thought you'd get a letter from me after all this time, hey, specially after that big fight we had. You should be so lucky, pal! (N.B. Note the above address. I'm just about the oldest inhabitant – four whole months, strewth, someone oughta give me a medal!)*

*So, how are things going with you? You learned to swim yet, you lazy nerd? I'm as well as can be expected (as the saying goes). I was going to nick off that many times when I first got here, you wouldn't have believed it. (Or maybe you would.) Once I hiked all the way to the nearest station, (like travelling over the Sahara Desert, no kidding). Just my terrific luck when I got there – next train wasn't due for another two hours! Nothing to look at except gum trees and I was feeling a bit wobbly and peculiar after that long walk. (Or maybe it was the baby giving me a good kick, who knows. It's obviously going to be a bit of a nagger, like you.) Anyhow, the thought of looking at gum trees for two hours didn't seem all that fantastic, so I turned round and came back here.*

*I'm staying on for a couple of months after the baby's born (got to make sure I'm really and truly recovered from flu and bronchitis and pleurisy and that!). Then we'll both be going to live with Mum and Dad for a bit. Back home.*

*I'm getting along fine, Seymour. (Honestly.) I
think maybe I'm going to make it this time
around. Just thought I'd tell you. When things
get a bit tough I go for walks – only not in the
direction of the railway station. The lake's full of
little silver fishes. (THEY can swim, you dill, so
why can't YOU?) They're so pretty to watch I
sit there for hours on end. It's peaceful.*

*I didn't get around to thanking you for
bringing Juliet for me that day, did I? Well,
thanks. She got a bit battered the first few weeks
here. I used to get so depressed I'd scrunch her
up in a ball and practically chew bits out of her.
But that part's all over now. I made her a new
dress and new plaits of wool and washed and
ironed and starched her. She just sits on my
dressing table now, looks like a new woman!*

*The baby's going to be fine, too, the doctor
said. They did this ultrasound – that's kind of
like a moving x-ray picture – and I saw its little
feet and it moved a hand and sort of waved to
me. God, it's so tiny, though you won't think so
from the photo I'm putting in with this letter. I
look like I'm going to have triplets!*

*Seymour, it won't ever be crying in its cot
because I've fallen asleep, truly it won't. You
don't ever have to worry about that now.*

*You should see all the cute things I've knitted
for it (while I'm down talking to the fish in the
lake).*

*I hope you get this letter and you haven't
moved on to some place else. And that things*

turned out OK for you at the new school and no one's giving you a hard time. You know I never meant it when I said I never liked you. That was just me feeling sorry for myself and hitting out at the nearest thing which just happened to be you. I thought you were an ace kid (even though you wore that daggy shirt!). I hope I see you again some day. Hey, how about writing to me? It gets a bit lonely up here. Sounds silly, doesn't it, when there are so many people here – sometimes we even have to have two shifts for meals in the dining room. But it's spooky, like climbing a big mountain all by yourself in the fog. Still, I reckon I'm nearly up to the top, now. When I get there, I'll tell you what the view's like!*

Love from Angie

* If Morris Carpenter's got anything to do with it, the fog might be just as thick up at the top! (Joke.)

PS. Please write to me, love. I really miss you. Be my friend, keep me comforty, OK?

# POSTSCRIPT

Dear Angie,

I got your letter and the photo – it was great to hear from you! Lots of times I wanted to write, but I didn't even know where you were – could have been Saturn for all I knew. Angie, I'm glad it's not.

Carrucan's not as bad as I thought it would be. My mum seems to like it, too. Her job was only supposed to be for six months, but the other lady went overseas. We've got a really beaut flat underneath the house and Mum bought me some wallpaper to do up my room. I've got posters and that stuck up, too. You should see it. Mum sort of bosses the old bloke who owns the house around a lot, but he's pretty deaf and doesn't seem to mind. He really likes her cooking and the way she keeps the house looking so tidy. I reckon we might be staying put for awhile.

Hey, guess what, I've got a terrific job here in Carrucan, two days a week after school and all day Saturdays. There's this kid at school I've got friendly with, Martin, and his dad runs a plant nursery. Mart and me get paid for watering the plants and carrying things out to people's cars and stuff like that. I even got a promotion yesterday at where I work. Marty's dad says, 'Hey, Seymour, you're such a good worker, I'm moving you on to bigger and better things.' I say, 'Wow! What?' He says, 'You can stack all those bags of fertiliser in the shed today instead of sweeping the paths.' (!!)

He's OK, though. We went to this airforce

show last weekend, it was unreal!

Angie, I'm glad you went to Lakeview and you didn't nick off. I'm glad you're staying there till the baby's born. I used to get these dreams, you know, about how you'd manage and what it would be like. They were pretty awful.

Anyhow, you can't very well nick off anywhere in your condition, can you? Honest, I didn't laugh at the photo you sent. You look OK in it, Ange. You look nice. I like that name you gave that dress, too, Barnum Bros Circus. It suits you looking . . . well, sort of chubby.

This present I'm sending – I carved it out of soapstone. Sorry the horses are a funny shape – Mart reckons they look more like flying kangaroos, but he helped me stick the hook things on the backs. You don't have to wear them if you think they're weird, but you like daggy earrings, so maybe you'll like these.

My dad came down to see me a couple of months ago. It was all right this time, he stayed in the motel and took me out a few times. He's got some kind of job with a mate of his who drives a truck, so he'll be moving around a fair bit. He says he'll send a postcard from all the different places. At least now he knows where to send it! I hope Carrucan's going to last longer than all those other places. I think it will.

Mart and me go down the pool a lot, it's a heated one here. I still can't swim very well, but I can sort of get around in the water now without drowning.

Let's know as soon as the baby comes, and when you get back home, we'll take it to the zoo to see the orang-outang. Lots of places we can take it.

You hang right in there, Angie!

Love from Seymour.

P.S. At the airforce show they were handing out things like showbags, and they had these little silver badges in them (well, not silver, I guess, only plastic). They're like those badges people get when they learn to fly. When you get back home, maybe I'll give it to you as a medal. But I'll have to wait and see.